Mary Pruyn

Grandmama's Letters from Japan

Mary Pruyn

Grandmama's Letters from Japan

ISBN/EAN: 9783337170981

Printed in Europe, USA, Canada, Australia, Japan

Cover: Foto ©Andreas Hilbeck / pixelio.de

More available books at **www.hansebooks.com**

GRANDMAMMA'S

LETTERS FROM JAPAN.

BY

MRS. MARY PRUYN.

––––––––––

BOSTON:
JAMES H. EARLE, PUBLISHER,
20 HAWLEY STREET.
1877.

CONTENTS.

I.

VII.

VIII.

IX.

X.

XI.

XII.

XIII.

XIV.

XV.

XVI.

XVII.

XVIII.

XIX.

XX.

PREFACE.

I NOT only love and believe in children, but I have something of a prophetic spirit with reference to their future influence, and I often find myself looking forward with earnest expectancy to results which shall be achieved through their faith and love.

I look back to my own childhood days, and remember with what avidity I seized and improved the few opportunities I had for gaining instruction concerning missionary work; and I recall most vividly the earnest desires awakened, even when a little child, to be permitted to go and tell the heathen about Jesus. For forty years, those desires could find their only outlet in work among the children, the poor, and the outcast at home; then God called me, so distinctly that I could not doubt it was His voice, to go forth to a heathen land, and carry out into practical effect those early longings of my heart; but I have constantly felt that the impulse given to my mind before I was ten years old was the beginning of my preparation for the new and arduous but delightful work given me to do, when more than half a century of years had passed over my head.

When I left my home, I knew that not only in its loved circle, but in Sabbath and Industrial schools, there were many dear children who followed me with warm and loving interest, and to whom the missionary cause assumed a new significance because of my connection with it; and I was often cheered by the little messengers that came from them in my far-off island home, saying, "We pray for you and your work." It was pleasant recreation to send back to them occasional letters, not only to assure them of my love and remembrance, but to give them such information concerning the people and the country of Japan, as should excite their sympathy, and encourage them to some practical efforts to help in the good work there.

The letters were generally written hurriedly, and without the faintest idea that other eyes than those to whom they were addressed would ever see them. There is no attempt at order, or thoroughness in them, and they were usually suggested by some passing incident. Certainly there is no merit in them, beyond their truthfulness and simplicity. Yet in looking them over, it has been rather urgently suggested by kind and perhaps partial friends that they contain many things that would interest Sabbath-school children, and might serve to give some minds the same impulses that so early stirred my own.

With the consent of the little folks to whom they were written, — the most of them my grandchildren, — I have gathered up some of those letters, and in precisely the simple and familiar style in which they were written to my own dear little ones, I send them out to the children of our Sabbath schools and Christian families.

When I was quite a little child I was taken to New York, and while there accompanied my brother to a great Fair of the American Institute, held in what was then a very fashionable place, called Niblo's Garden. Upon a large table stood a fine glass case, around which many persons were gathered, all anxious to see the wonderful things it contained. My brother made inquiries of many persons, but all he could learn was this : "Far off in some part of the world there was a place called Japan. No one could tell anything about the country, or the people, except they were very strange, and only once a year would allow a few Dutch traders to come there and buy some of their curious goods." In that case were some of their beautiful things, brought away by some Dutchmen, and sold to an American merchant, who was exhibiting them as great curiosities that had come all the way from that strange and almost unknown land. What a change has come since that day ! I suppose not one of the dear children who may read these letters is as ignorant now as the wise and grown-up men were when my brother questioned them. Japan is now our nearest heathen neighbor, and travellers from our country, and from all lands, are constantly going there to see for themselves the strange people, and the wondrously beautiful country. The rich and elegant wares from Japan are freely sold to any one who desires them, and have found their way into the homes of wealth and refinement in every civilized land, while the history of the country has become so incorporated in the text-books of our schools, that even our little children are becoming familiar with it.

But more, and far better, Christian people are to-day doing all they can to give the precious gospel to that nation, and God has so blessed their efforts that already churches and Sabbath schools are springing up all over the country. May He speed the time when the Bible shall be there, as it is in our own beloved land, the foundation of a true religious liberty, and when all the children of Japan shall grow up in the knowledge of our Lord and Saviour Jesus Christ.

And may He grant His blessing upon this little book, so that these simple letters may go to the hearts of many American children as His message, calling some of them to go work in that part of His vineyard, and awakening in all of them some earnest desires to have a part in the labor at home, by which others shall be sent to establish in those beautiful islands the kingdom of our glorious King.

M. P.

ALBANY, N. Y., August, 1876.

LETTERS FROM JAPAN.

I.

TWELVE HUNDRED MILES AT SEA,
June 6, 1871.

TO MY DEAR LITTLE FOLKS AT HOME, —
MARY, BERTIE, AND KITTIE:

I just wish you could look at me as I sit here in this beautiful cabin of the good ship Japan, and feel with me the pure, fresh sea-air, as it blows so cool and delightful over me; or if you could go with me out on the deck, and look over the great Pacific Ocean, on which we are sailing, how you would wonder!

Can you think of being in a place where you can see nothing but water? If I go to one end of the ship, and look away off as far as I can see, there is only water; if I go to the other end, it is just the same: water all around us, and sky all above us. No trees; no houses; no people, except those on the ship with us. This ship is a very large one, and has people enough on it now to make a good-sized village, but it does not seem at all crowded.

There are a good many little children with us, and I think the captain must be very fond of little people, for he has put up a nice swing on the upper deck for them, and seems pleased to see them happy and playful. But it is a very long time for them to be shut up in one place; it will be three weeks before the ship will reach Japan, and it is pretty hard to be contented and quiet so long, — do not you think so?

All the waiters and servants are a

strange-looking people. They come from China, which is a country very far away— even farther than Japan is from America. I am sure you would laugh to see them, they are so odd. They are all men, but they do women's work just as nicely as though they wore dresses. All the hair is shaved off their heads, except a small round spot on the top; that is allowed to grow very long, and in with it they braid a large quantity of coarse black sewing-silk, so that when it is newly fixed it makes a long, glossy braid that hangs down nearly to their heels.

It is curious to see thirty or forty of these fellows running about, waiting upon the table, with these long tails swinging and flying around, every step they take! Then they wear the queerest kind of shoes, that turn up at the toes, and look just like little boats on their feet; with long white stockings and short blue pants. . . . I cannot tell you all the wonderful things I am seeing since I came from home, but I think you will hear a good deal from my other letters, and I will try and write to you before very long.

Now there is something I want you to do for me. Every time you pray at night, I want you to ask God to help me do a great deal for the little children of Japan, so they may learn to love Him, as I think you do. You know these poor children have never heard of our dear Lord Jesus, and they do not know how good He is, nor how much He loves them. This is what I want to teach them, and you can pray for me. I know God hears little children, and it will make me very happy to be sure that you pray for His blessing.

Ever your loving

GRANDMOTHER.

II.

YOKOHAMA, July 2, 1871.

MY DEAR MARY:

This is Sabbath morning with us, but in Albany it is only Saturday evening, for you know we are in the East, though I came west to reach here, which seems very strange, — does it not? Some time I will explain this to you; or you can ask your papa to tell you how it is. But, any way, I cannot think of you now as getting ready to go to Sunday school, as you would be, I hope, on the precious Sabbath morning. When our evening comes, and our time for going to bed arrives, then I will think you are in Sunday school, and learning something more about Jesus and God's holy word. When I think of my dear children at home, and all their comforts and privileges, it makes me sad to look upon the children in this heathen city, and see how different is their life, without the Bible or the knowledge of our dear Jesus.

It seems very strange to me here on the Sabbath. There are a few Christians, who have come from other countries, and they keep God's holy day; but none of the native people know anything about His command "Remember the Sabbathday to keep it holy," and most of those who have come from Christian lands are so wicked that they do not care any more for it than the heathen do; and so there is very little difference here between this and any other day. The people all keep their stores open; they go out with their boats to fish; they work in their

fields and gardens, and carry things about
to sell, just as they do on other days. O,
it makes me so sorry, and I would so
love to tell them of our dear Father in
heaven, who has given us the Sabbath
for our happiness! but they speak such
a strange language, I cannot talk with
them, or make them understand anything
about it. Some good men are working
very hard to put the Bible into the Japanese language, and when that is done,
they can read of Jesus, and what God,
the true God, would have them do.

There are so many little children here,
and, O, I do pray that before they grow
up, the Bible will be all ready for them,
for I want them to become Christian men
and women, and not idolaters as their
parents are! The children here are the
best-natured and most contented and happy little things I ever saw; though I am

sure you would wonder how they could be, if you should see them. If you had to live in such poor little houses, wear such poor, miserable clothes, or perhaps not wear any, as is the case with many of them, you would think it very hard. But they do not seem to mind it, and play about all day without crying or quarrelling at all. I have never seen any of them that even looked as if they felt cross: do you not think little Christian children could learn something from them in this? I do; and I am sure I could not wish my little folks to be more kind and pleasant with each other than are these heathen children.

You know we are going to have a school to teach the children and young girls to read, and about our God; and yesterday a gentleman said to me, "Such a school will be a god-send to these peo-

ple;" and that is just what I think too:
God did send us here, and I am sure He
will help us to do them good. Some
time I will tell you about their houses,
and dress, and playthings; but this is all
to-day from

GRANDMA.

III.

YOKOHAMA, Aug. 26, 1871.

MY DEAR GRANDCHILDREN :

I have written to mamma all about our moving into this house, and what a terrible storm we had just after we got here: these storms are called *typhoons*, and are very frequent in the East during the summer and fall; but I want to tell you a little incident connected with it, which I think will interest you.

I have mentioned that little Carrie and Annie B—— came to stay with us while their papa and mamma went up on the mountains; and on that morning, when the storm became so very violent, we could not stop for our morning prayers

or breakfast: yet we all felt that our only
hope of safety was in God's power to keep
us from harm. As I went into my room
for something, I saw dear little Carrie on
her knees. I passed out quietly, but in a
few moments she came to me and said,—

"We did not have prayers this morning."

"No," I replied, "we could not stop,
on account of the storm; but you know
we can pray while we are working, and
I have a good many times asked God to
take care of us."

"Yes," she said, "I know that; but I
had no work to do, so I went and prayed;
and I told God He was the only One who
could help us, and I asked Him *for
Christ's* sake to do it. Then I told Jesus
He had *promised* that *anything* we
asked for His sake should be done, and
I know He will do it."

Was it not very sweet? I hope you will remember this. How much that little child's faith had to do with our preservation during that awful storm, who can tell? . . .

From your loving

GRANDMAMMA.

IV.

YOKOHAMA, Nov. 2, 1871.

DEAR MARY, BERTIE, AND KITTIE:

If I could write all I think, you would
have a great many very long letters from
grandma; but then I am afraid you
would get tired reading them, and so
perhaps it is better for your mamma to
read some of her letters to you, and by
them you will know what is going on
away off here in Japan. To-day I am
going to tell you some good news, which
I am sure you will be glad to hear; and
that is, we have now quite a number of
little children in our family, and a few
young ladies; besides, there are a good
many young men who come to this house
every day to study English.

The people here are very anxious to learn our language, and they will do anything to get such knowledge; and though they do not yet care about our religion, they are very willing to read in the Bible when they are here. This makes us all so glad, for we know that God's Word contains the true wisdom, and if they read it, they must learn something of our God, and how good and loving He is; and then we feel sure they will not want to worship any longer their ugly wooden and stone gods.

It seems very strange that any people can believe that such hideous old images as their gods are, can do anything for them. I went to an old temple, the other day, that is about six hundred years old, — older than our country, a great deal, — and I wish I had time to write you of all the strange old things I saw there. I will tell you of a few. First, — and what pained me most, — the greatest crowd of all kinds of people thronged about us as we went through the street in the old town of Kanagawa. It is not very often they see a foreigner, and they are so curious whenever one comes among them. They were so dirty, and had so little clothing on, that I did not like to look at them. Then so many of the children were all covered with sores: O, it was pitiful!

As we went up to the temple, we passed under a large stone gateway, or Tori, which is always placed before all their temples. Then on each side of the building, on the outside, are two large wooden images, which are placed there as guardians of the gods. Is it not a strange idea that gods need to be guarded? These figures are the most horrid-looking creatures you can imagine. They are always made sixteen feet high, and painted a bright red. They have their eyes staring wide, and their mouths open, showing their teeth, and altogether look so hideous and ferocious that I do not wonder they think evil spirits are afraid to come near them.

When the people go to the temple to pray, they carry with them some small pieces of paper, which they get from the priests, and on which are written a few characters. When they come near these images, they chew one of these papers up into a small ball, and throw it at the "guardian." If it sticks fast, then they believe the gods in the temple will hear their prayers, and they go in; and after putting a few cash, or pennies, into the box near the door, they go up to the altar and pray before the gods. If these little balls fall off, they think it is no use to pray that day, and so they do not go in. Those figures I saw before the temple were all covered over with these little "spit-balls," and I was told that sometimes the priest has to go to work and scrape them all off, to make room for more.

Inside the temple there were more gods than I could count, and many of the altars looked very much like those you can see in the Catholic churches in Albany. Indeed, there is a great deal in the worship of these idolaters that is so nearly like the Romish church, that one could almost believe they were the same. One thing is peculiar here. The floors are all covered over with white mats, and there are no seats. The Japanese do not use any chairs, and at home, and in their temples, sit right upon the floor.

There are no Sundays for them, but

3

they have what they call "Matsuris," or
Festival days, and then every one is ex-
pected to go to their own temple, give a
little money, and say some prayers; besides this, all the temples have a good
many priests, who live in them, and are
always ready to say prayers for any who
come there. So that there is no time when
there are not priests and people in the
temple. No one is allowed to go in with
shoes on their feet, so we had to sit on
the outside steps and take ours off.

But my letter is getting so long that I
must not tell you any more, except a short
story about "Georgie," one of our little
boys. He is a very quiet, gentle little fellow, eight years old. He is one of the very
brightest scholars we have, and is learning to understand and speak English very
rapidly. As I write, I hear him singing,
quite correctly, "I am glad I'm in this

army." You can scarcely imagine how much I enjoy listening to these dear children as they sing in the midst of their play, and at all times, snatches of our sweet Sunday-school hymns. Georgie's father died, and left him, with his little brother, who is also with us, to the care of their heathen mother. She is very glad to have them here, and seems quite proud to have them learn so readily; but still she wants them to worship her gods, and never loses an opportunity to teach them to do so. A short time ago she came here and brought some of those little pieces of paper of which I have written. She told Georgie he must go to the temple to pray, and use them there. Until he came here, he had never known there was a better way to pray; but when she gave those papers to him, he said nothing, but walking very quietly to the other end of the veranda, he tore them all up into small bits, and then turning to Eddie, who stood near, he said, "I am going to pray to the true God." He wanted to obey his mother, but he could not dishonor the true God.

You cannot think how these little things rejoice my heart. I think they ought to make the friends at home feel that the bread they are casting upon these waters is found without waiting "many days." And this is some of the "good news" I told you I was going to write. I hope you will thank God for all He is doing; and that He may keep and bless my dear children away off in America, is the constant prayer of your

GRANDMOTHER.

V.

To the Teachers and Scholars of the
First Reformed S. S., Albany:

YOKOHAMA, Jan. 7, 1872.

Dear Friends: I thought we were coming to Japan to work for little children,
and when I last talked with you, this was
our intention and desire; yet we were
willing to do anything God gave us to
do. There is plenty of that kind of work
to do, and yet it is a little strange; and
if we were not so sure that God is lead-
ing us in His way, we might be troubled,
that we cannot seem to get at it, while
other work is crowding upon us. We
have been only four months in this house,
and yet in that time it is incredible how

many of these poor heathen have found their way here, and come asking for instruction. One of our ladies has made considerable progress in the language, and is able to teach them, partly in English and partly in Japanese. More than thirty, men, women, boys, and girls, come here daily, and more than the same number we have been compelled to deny. It is very hard to do this, when they beg to be allowed to come and "study the Holy Book," but one person cannot do more than our dear Mrs. P—— is doing.

Then we all feel that we should confine our efforts more exclusively to the women and girls, as the most proper and hopeful class for us to labor for.

Beside this, our house is very unsuitable for a large school, and we must have better accommodations to work to advantage; and just here, dear friends, is where

I want you to feel is your opportunity
to aid in this good cause. To procure
the land, and build such a house as we
need, will cost a great deal of money;
but when we have a suitable dwelling,
we can do a vast deal more than is possible now. We have had several appli-
cations to take young girls, and even ladies,
but were obliged to refuse for the want
of room.

More than this, we want more teachers. We want you to send some more
ladies, who can be learning the language,
and be ready to teach these people when
the government changes the laws, and
will allow them to learn, without the
fear of punishment. They must do this
soon, for the people are beginning to see
and feel the injustice of these laws, and
will not submit to them much longer.
The bold and courageous do not regard

them very much now, and are pressing
up and onward to the light; yet there are
many timid ones, and they are waiting,
secretly longing for the time to come.
The missionaries and Christian people
here, feel that it is very important to be
prepared for this liberty, and hence we
desire that there be many more here to
study the language.

I must not forget to tell you, that within the last few weeks a prayer-meeting
has been commenced in our house, by a
few natives who come here on Sabbath
evenings, at first to learn to sing; and
that now for the first time in the history
of this ancient empire, native Japanese
pray together, and exhort one another,
and that too with native women present.
Nor must I omit to tell you, that those
who come here daily for instruction have
nearly all learned the Lord's Prayer, and

repeat it at the opening of the school: and, better yet, several have asked to have a short prayer written for them, which they translate into their language, and offer in their own homes.

But I must tell you something of the dear little children who live in our home with us. We have five; and although they knew nothing of the dear Saviour, and had never been taught to pray, or sing His praise, yet I am sure it would delight your hearts, as it does mine, to hear them now. I think you will feel as I do, that we have cause to praise God, that in less than three months these dear children have learned to sing, "There is a happy land," "Jesus loves me;" can join in asking a blessing at the table, and repeat every morning and evening a little prayer we wrote for them, besides trying to say, "Our Father who art in heaven."

It made me so happy the other day to have one of our little girls tell me that Eddie had said, they must pray aloud in their rooms with each other; that he had begun, and they were to take their turn each morning.

In my lot, in the Albany Cemetery, is a little monument, on which is engraved the words "Eddie and Annie." Is it not a little singular that the two first heathen children committed to my care bear these names in the same order? My own precious ones

> " Have gone into that school
> Where they no longer
> Need my poor protection,
> And Christ himself doth rule."

Has He not sent these dear little ones to me, to be trained for the same blessed school? I believe He has, and it is a joy to me to hear them repeat over and over again, the first English words they learned to utter, "God is Love."

And now, dear friends and children, I hope I have told you enough to make you feel that it is not only a duty, but a great privilege to help in giving the gospel to these people, and in building a house where many can be gathered in, and trained up in the fear and love of God.

I am always yours,

In Christ's service,

MARY PRUYN.

VI.

YOKOHAMA, Feb. 26, 1872.

MY DEAR LITTLE FOLKS AT HOME:

As mamma and papa are away off in Georgia, I suppose I must consider *you* the family now, and send you a very big letter. . . . I am so glad to hear that you are trying to be such helpful children, and it pleased me very much to know that you are all so willing to deny yourselves candy, and many little things that children love so well, that you may have more pennies to put in your "mite boxes." We expect to build a large house soon, which will cost a great deal of money, and then we will want a good deal more to furnish it nicely; but I think if you, and all the little friends in America, could see the little Japanese children who come here every day to school, you would love them, and think it a great pleasure to help get a nice house and school-room for them. They are not handsome, and they look very odd, but they are very quiet and obedient, and they all seem so anxious to learn, that it is no trouble to take care of them, or to make them study.

But I want to tell you in this letter something about the Japanese New Year, which is just past, for you see they do not have it the same time we do. You will think this very strange, but then you must remember that for hundreds of years this country has been so shut up, that no one knew what was going on in other parts of the world, and they did not know or care what other people were doing. So, when foreign people began to come here, a few years ago, they found many things just as they had been for centuries, and very different from other places; for while all the civilized countries had been changing and advancing very fast, Japan had been, as it were, asleep, and everything was standing still. This is one reason why their year does not begin at the same time ours does; but I think it will not be long before they change the time, for they are getting awake now, and they want to be like the rest of the world.

Well, to tell you about it. The new year always comes in the month we call February, but the exact day is regulated by the moon. The festival of the new year is a very important one, and always lasts a whole week. They give presents and make visits just as we do at home, and some people think our custom came from Japan; that it was learned from them by the Holland people who used to go there to trade, many hundred years ago, and by them taken to Holland, and then brought from there to America. I cannot tell how true this is, but it is a little odd to find these people doing exactly as we have always been accustomed to do in this respect, and it is very pleasant and natural for me, I can assure you.

The houses here are so small that the people live about as much in the streets as they do in-doors; and at this time, as you go about the town, everything looks gay and lively. Each one is dressed in his or her best clothes; and, indeed, every one who expects to have them at all during the year, has *new* ones; for these poor folks do not generally get anything new except at this season.

Very little work is done during this

week, but all sorts of plays and amuse-
ments are going on. The chief of these
are, for the girls, dolls, for the boys,
kites, and shuttlecock for all. Though I
might say *all*, about each kind of these
toys or plays, for the men and women
seem nearly as fond of them as the children are, and all over the streets you see
them busy, either using these things themselves, or helping the little ones.

The kites they use are very funny
things: they all have some peculiar shape.
Some like a great head of a man, or beast;
some a cow, or a bird; or, what they seem
very fond of, a demon, or evil spirit. You
cannot think how curious and odd they
look, and how much they appear like the
real object they represent, when they are
away up in the air, floating about above
you. Then, many of them have a queer
device fastened in them, that sounds, as

JAPANESE WOMAN PLAYING WITH A DOLL.

(From a Photograph.)

the air rushes through it, just like a soft, musical whistle; and when there are a good many of them around, it is strange, but really very pleasant, to hear, so far up towards the clouds, the music they make. Our little children have some that I bought for them, and they think it great fun to send them off up in the air.

Then, the dolls of Japan are quite an institution, and are the funniest things imaginable. They look so like real babies and children, that I have often been deceived when I have seen them in the arms, carried about the streets. Besides playing with dolls at New Year's time, and any other, when they choose, there are two days set apart in April for what is called a "Doll's Festival," and all the girls, and even big women, make a great time of it. They take them out to walk, and visit, and get new dresses for them, and treat them just as tenderly as if they were live children.

You may think it funny for women to do this, but you do not know that the women in Japan are not taught to work, or spend their time in any useful way. There are no schools for girls, and so they grow up without learning anything that can fill their minds with good thoughts, or help them to pass their time pleasantly. The poor Japanese women have a very aimless life, and I think playing with dolls is about as harmless a way for them to get pleasure as they could find.

Another thing that is peculiar to the new year is the way the houses are ornamented. Before every house small bamboo trees are set up; and as the leaves of these are small, and of a beautiful light green, and wave prettily in the breeze, they make the dark and small houses appear quite cheerful and bright as one looks along the street. Then, all along the front eaves of the houses they hang a deep fringe, made of straw, which also waves with every breath of wind, and looks odd and handsome. Another device is so very peculiar, and so much a part of the superstitious character of the people, that I must try and tell you about it.

They place near the front of the house (and you know all their houses are made entirely open along the front, only closed at night, and in great storms, by sliding doors) a large pile, or pyramid, of cooked rice; on the top of this they put some fine straw, then some bitter oranges, next a crab, and, on top of all, a piece of dried fish-skin.

The meaning of all is this: The rice

represents the "Island of eternal happiness," which they think lies somewhere
off in the ocean, and to which they desire
to go when they die. The straw is a
protection from evil spirits. The orange
is to them an emblem of successive gen-
erations. By this they tell their gods that
they wish themselves, and all their children, of every generation, to go to that
island, but they also want to be pro-
tected from the bad spirits while they
live here. The crab expresses their desire to live till they are so old that they
will have to creep along, all doubled up.
And then, the fish-skin is always used by
them, in all their presents and salutations,
to express politeness and good wishes,
and so they desire the gods to receive
their reverence and good will, while they
grant all their desires.

Does not all this show you how dark

their minds are, and that while they are
groping after future happiness, they know
little of the wonderful gift of our God,
even eternal life, through Jesus Christ?

But this is a very long letter, and now
I must close. Only I want to tell you
that nothing pleases me so much as to
hear that you pray for me every day, and
that God will make this school the place
where many will come to learn the truth,
and forsake their foolish customs. I am
sure God is already answering your
prayers, and that is the reason why we
have such a happy home, and so much
to praise Him for.

As ever, I am your affectionate

GRANDMOTHER.

VII.

YOKOHAMA, April 18, 1872.

MY DEAR KITTIE:

I want to tell you about one of our little girls whom we call Nona, though that is not her real name. Her father came from another country, and has plenty of money, but, like a great many people in this wicked city who have come from Christian lands, he is a bad man, and drinks so much liquor that he does not care for anybody or anything; though, when he is sober, he seems to love his little girl, and is willing to pay well to have her taken care of here.

She had a wicked heathen mother, and when little Nona was only three years old, she went away, and left her with a careless, bad girl; so for a year and a half the poor little thing had a very hard life, and suffered much for the want of some kind friends. What has been the hardest is, that through the carelessness of those who were with her, she was hurt very badly, and one foot and leg is so much injured that she cannot walk alone; and though it will get better, we hope, by good treatment, yet she will never be able to run about, and skip, and jump like other children.

Well, this little one came to us about five months ago. She could not speak, or understand a word of English, and had never heard of God, or such a thing as singing. I think I have told you that the Japanese never sing, and it is only since Christian people have come here that they have heard it. It was quite amusing to see little Nona's wonder and interest when she first heard us singing hymns, and I knew at once that she was going to make a good singer herself. She had a very bad temper, and at first it was very difficult to make her obey; but God helped us to govern her, and she soon learned to do as she was told.

I wish you could see and hear her now, as I often do, when she comes down into the dining-room, early in the morning, and sits there waiting for the other children and the breakfast. She likes to get up early, and is generally the first one to come down stairs. There she will sit in her little chair, so contented and happy, and sing one hymn after another, "Jesus loves me," "Christ is born the Lord of glory," "There is a happy land," and parts of several others; and then when the breakfast is over, she claims a cushion beside me, while we read our morning Bible lesson; and, kneeling at the same chair with me, she always repeats, with us, the Lord's prayer, at the end of our worship. And it is the most touching thing to me sometimes, when I am praying, to feel her little hand working itself into mine, or softly laid against my cheek.

And this little creature, so apt, so affectionate, was, five months ago, a poor, neglected little waif, floating about among the most degraded heathen. Do you not love her, my dear little Kittie, and are you not glad she has now such a pleasant home, and some one to tell her of Jesus and his love?

Good-by, for to-day, from

GRANDMA.

VIII.

YOKOHAMA, May 15, 1872.

MY DEAR MARY:

This is the anniversary of my leaving
you in dear old Albany, and I might feel
very sad, as I think of the great distance
between my home and dear ones, and the
long year that has passed since I saw
them, but God has been so good, and so
many things have happened during this
past year to make me glad and thankful,
that I will not allow myself to be one bit
sad to-day. And to make the time pass
pleasantly, and give you something that
I think will interest you, I am going to
tell you of an excursion I made into the
country. This will help you to under-

stand how the Japanese live, and something of their strange ways.

I went with Mr. B—— and his two little daughters, and Ogowa and his wife, two nice Japanese Christians. The people over on the other side of the bay had heard something about the teachings of the missionaries in Yokohama, and they sent a man over to Ogowa, whose home used to be over there, to ask him if he would bring a Christian teacher there, who could tell them about Jesus. We all thought it a very wonderful thing, and felt sure it was an answer to the prayers that are constantly being offered, that the Holy Spirit will incline the hearts of this people to receive the truth. That was the reason Mr. B—— and Ogowa went, and as they wanted me to go along, I concluded to do so.

We all started to sail in a Japanese

boat across the bay, and it was a very
funny experience, I can tell you. Their
little boats are queer things, and very
unlike anything you have at home. Then,
the wind blew very hard, and some of
us, myself among the number, were so
sea-sick that we had to lie right down
in the bottom of the boat, among the
ropes and boards, and, O, we did feel so
bad, we thought we never could get up
to go on shore when the boat reached
the other side!

All that passed away, however, as soon
as the boat became still; but what do
you think we found when we stopped
sailing? Why, that we were nearly a
mile from the land! The boat stuck fast
in the sand, and could not get any nearer,
because the water was not deep enough.
This was a pretty fix, — do you not think
so? Well, the people here did not seem

to mind it much, for they are used to it;
and so the coolies, or "Sendos," as they
call the sailors, got over the sides of the
boat into the water, which was about two
feet deep, and said they would carry us
on their backs.

This cured me of my sea-sickness very
soon, for I had to laugh so much to see
how the others were all carried; but I
would not try it that way. I told Mr.
B—— if he would show two men how
to make a chair with their arms (you
know how that is done — do you not?)
I would sit on that, but I would never
ride astride a man's back.

Well, they tried it, by Mr. B——'s
direction, and I started very nicely; but
when I got about half-way to the shore,
I found they were getting very unsteady,
and at last they let me slide right down
into the water. I laughed so hard that

for a while I could not walk, but at last
I went on, and waded the rest of the
way, and finally got safely to the dry
land, where all the rest were standing
laughing at me. I learned a good lesson
by it, and hereafter I do not mean to set
myself up to be wiser and better than
every one else, but just do as others do,
and make the best of it.

When we came on shore, a crowd of
dirty, curious people, including children,
gathered about us; and you will not wonder they did so, when I tell you that I
was the first white or foreign woman
who had ever been in that part of the
country.

After some delay we got a "Norimono"
for me to ride in, and horses for the rest
of the party, and started off for the place
back in the country where we had been
invited. A Norimono is a square box,

about three feet high, and nearly as long;
just wide enough for one person to sit
in.   It is all enclosed, and one has to sit
upon the feet "tailor-fashion."   A pole is
fastened along the top, by which two men
carry it on their shoulders.   It is pleasant at first, but very soon one gets tired
sitting so cramped up, and then the
swinging motion makes one feel almost
as bad as when sea-sick.

In going out, we passed through a
beautiful part of the country, and I saw
how the farmers live, and cultivate their
land.   Many things were very odd, and
I would like to describe them, but only
a few can I tell you about.   They plant
a great deal of rice all over Japan, for
that is the principal article of food.   The
people never eat bread, as we do, and
rice serves instead.   These rice-fields are
always kept covered with water, and so,

5

to get places to plant other things in, — such as potatoes, beans, radishes, &c., — they throw up little patches or squares of earth, making them about three feet higher than the rice and water, and on the top of them they plant all those things. It looks very pretty but curious, as you ride along, to see these little square places, all over the country, covered with such different-colored vegetation from that growing down on the level of the ground.

Then they have such a strange way of training pear-trees. They plant them in long rows, quite close together, and as they grow up about seven or eight feet high, they begin to turn the branches all crosswise, and tie them to one another. By the time the trees get to be a pretty good size, it looks underneath like a long hall, or passage-way, with very regular col-

umns upon each side, and a thick, rich
ceiling of beautiful green leaves overhead. Looking down upon one of the
large pear orchards, you can see nothing
but a solid green floor. They always
take a great deal of pains to have them
kept nicely trimmed, and really they are
most beautiful, though the fruit is not at
all nice, as it never gets any sun, which
you know is very necessary.

The gentleman at whose house we
stayed is like the "Patroon" of Albany.
He is very rich, and has hundreds of
retainers. These are not exactly servants, but still they are governed and
supported by him. The place is very
large, and is surrounded by a moat, or
canal, which is to prevent any enemies
from getting in. We crossed a large
stone bridge, and, going through a mas-
sive gate-way, found ourselves in an immense open square, around which were a

great many houses, some large and some small, but all pretty and neat.

We then, after crossing this square, passed through another gate, not so large, but much more elegant, and entered the garden of our host. This was wondrously beautiful. There were little lakes and waterfalls, miniature mountains, caves, grottos, bridges, with all kinds of trees, trained to represent ships, houses, dogs, and birds. You could hardly believe how perfect they can make the shape of these objects out of the evergreen trees that grow here.

We were received in the house very politely, but many things were not according to our ideas, and we would think some things quite rude; yet, as we knew these people did not mean it so, we tried not to notice their strange ways.

One thing we have to bear in every place, and we found the rich people just as much given to it as the poor — that is, a curiosity to examine everything you wear, or carry with you.

The Japanese people do not use beds like ours, but lie upon the floor, with just one very heavy covering over them, and a wooden block for a pillow. We could not use such pillows, so we had brought with us some sheets and pillows of our own. We could not eat their kind of food, and we had packed up a parcel of canned meat, and fruits, and also some bread, butter, cakes, &c.

As we opened our parcels, it was very amusing to see how curious the people were, from the host and his aged mother, down to the tiny children of the servants, for all gathered about us to see. In a Japanese gentleman's house, the servants and their children seem just as free and familiar as any members of the family; and although they are always very respectful, and know their proper place, they are treated with so much kindness that one can hardly tell if they are servants or not.

I was almost sorry we had brought our own food, for the gentleman was so polite, and anxious to do everything he could for us; but, although it seemed rude in us, it was really necessary, for, excepting eggs, chickens, fish, and potatoes, there is nothing we can eat now; perhaps by and by we may learn to like their strange ways of cooking.

But my letter has grown so long that I think I must not try to tell you about the rest of our visit this time. When I write again, perhaps I will finish the story; for many things happened which I thought very pleasant and interesting.

Now I will only say, "God bless all my dear little ones in America."

GRANDMA.

IX.

YOKOHAMA, June 20, 1872.

MY DEAR GRANDCHILDREN:

I wonder if my dear little children at home would not like to spend a little time with grandma to-day, and listen to some stories about these strange people in this far-off place. Well, I take this for granted, as big folks say; but since you cannot do this, because a great ocean rolls between us, I am going to try and have a little talk with my pen. I often thank our dear Father in heaven that we have pen and paper, and that I learned to use them, and have eyes to see how to write, so that, although I am so far from all my dear ones, I can still tell them so easily the thoughts that are in my heart. Do you ever thank God for your little, common, every-day comforts? Do you not think it pleases Him when we try to see His love and tender care for us in all the good things we have, whether they are great or small?

But I am going to tell you now about a great religious festival that is going on among the Chinese and Japanese here. There are a good many Chinese in this place, and it seems this festival is kept by the people of this country and those of China at the same time, although their religion is not exactly the same.

I cannot find out just the precise object of these observances, but, as near as I can learn, they are intended in some way to help the spirits of all their friends who are dead. Something, I think, as the Catholic people do when they pray for the dead; only these heathen seem to think that their dead friends need something for the body as well as for the spirit. Our servants, who try to use all the English they can, call all their religious seasons "Sundays," and they say this is "big Sunday." It has lasted three days, and closes to-night.

In all the temples they have bells suspended — or, rather, in a little outside building: these bells are made of bronze, and the sound is produced by striking on them with a hammer. In every direction these bells have been sounding all these days. They have a peculiar but very musical sound, and that, together with the fire-crackers, which are used very profusely by the Chinese, makes it seem almost like our Fourth of July.

The Chinese who live here are, like all of that race, very proud, and think themselves a great deal better than the Japanese; and it quite vexes me sometimes to see them treat the poor Japs as though they were no better than dogs.

The lot on which this house stands, like all the lots on this bluff, is of very irregular shape, and the back part of it runs down a steep, almost perpendicular hill. Adjoining the very lowest part of it is a Chinese burying-ground, and one day they had some very strange ceremonies there. There was no one to explain them to us, and so I cannot tell you what they mean; and it was all so funny that I would have felt like laughing at it, only it made me realize how ignorant and blind the poor creatures are, and I felt, since it was a part of their superstitious religion, I ought rather to pity them.

I suppose very nearly all the Chinese in the city were assembled in the grave-

yard, dressed in white — white is their
color for mourning — or light-blue garments : loose, flowing coats, and baggy
trousers reaching only to the knees; long,
white stockings, queer, boat-like shoes,
bare heads, and their long black pigtails
hanging down their backs.

They had brought there several large
baskets, very much like the crates crock-
ery comes packed in. On the ground,
in various places, they spread large straw
mats. Then they put up in rows, all
around the grounds, little sticks about a
foot and a half high, which I think was
punk, such as you light fire-crackers
with, for they lighted them all, and they
burned very slowly for many hours; or
they might have been incense sticks, for
they placed one at the head and one at
the foot of every grave.

Then they took out of one of the

crates two large trays, and two whole roasted pigs, weighing at least one hundred pounds each. These pigs seemed to be skinned, and then covered all over with a kind of red plaster. They were placed on the trays, with all four of their legs bent under them, and then little dishes of boiled rice, cakes, and many kinds of fruit were arranged around them on the large mats, upon which each of the trays were set. They had ribbons and colored papers, too, in great profusion, put about and on them. Out of the other crate, or basket, they took a great quantity of small baskets, containing fruits and cakes, which they distributed all over the grounds.

In a large, white structure, which I had often noticed, and thought was a monument, but which proved to be a hollow oven, they made a great fire, and smaller ones on the ground near the pigs. Then each person took a small teacup, and poured into it, from a great can that stood there, some liquid, which I guess was tea; this they would throw into the fires, and then kneeling upon the mats near by, they prostrated themselves entirely to the ground, touching it with their foreheads every time they bent over, while they threw their arms out and backward in a wild and singular manner.

After this they made long rows of what looked like pieces of white paper; but they must have been a kind of fire-cracker, for as they set fire to one end of the row, it ran along the whole line, popping and snapping with a tremendous noise.

From our back windows we watched them with our opera-glasses, and could distinctly see every movement. It was a curious but painful sight to me. I could only surmise, from what I know of heathen superstitions, that the food was designed to supply the wants of the dead in the other world, and the papers burned were prayers for their happiness. I rather think the whole thing was intended for the benefit of those who are in the other world, and is done every year to prove their affection and reverence for their departed friends.

The ceremony of burning the papers has been repeated three times during the week.

After the performance was over, all the articles of food were distributed among the servants and poor people, who had gathered in great numbers around the place. I was glad to see that done, and so some good came to them; but is it not strange the poor idolaters could suppose their dead friends received any benefit from it, when it was all eaten up by living people here?

You can hardly imagine what a sad and strange feeling it gives me to know that I am surrounded by those who are so totally ignorant of the true God, and Jesus Christ whom He has sent, — to be compelled to feel that *not one* of all this multitude knew anything of the only way by which they can obtain eternal life.

Sometimes, as I sit here by this dear little desk, in this quiet, pleasant room, I forget that I am in a heathen land, and so far from those scenes and persons I love so well; but a single glance out of the windows dispels all such illusions, and forces me to the painful conviction that it is true of this people what one of the holy men wrote in the Bible hundreds of years ago: "Darkness covers the

land, and gross darkness the people." It
is very comforting to see, however, that
light is beginning to break in. A few
are learning to read God's precious word,
and I feel very sure the time is not far
off when the truth will be freely taught
here.

Now, this is "grandma's talk" for to-
day. I hope it will please you; and while
you are sorry for these poor heathen
people, you will be very thankful that
you live in a Christian land.

Now, and always,

With warmest love,

GRANDMOTHER.

X.

YOKOHAMA, August 6, 1872.

DEAR MARY, BERTIE, AND KITTIE:

How I would like to see you walking about this house to-day! and how I would put my arms close, O, so close, around you, and kiss you so many, many times! Well, I cannot see you here, but you do not know how much I think about you, and how many things I see and hear that I would like to tell you of. O dear! if it did not take so long to write it all, how much you would hear from Japan! There are other dear children, too, to whom I would write if I could get the time; but since I cannot, I have been thinking that you could ask

6

your mamma or Aunt A—— to take this letter to the Industrial schools and read it to the children, and then it would please them too, and they would know that I think of them, though I am so far away.

I am going to tell you something more about the children in Japan, for I want you to know all you can of them, and I think you will like it as well as anything I can write. I do believe there are more children here, for the size of the country and the number of grown-up people, than there are anywhere else in the world.

It is very fortunate for those who live here that they are so good-natured and quiet, for it would be dreadful if they were as noisy and quarrelsome as some children I have seen. Some persons say they are so good because their parents allow them to do just as they choose.

Now, I dare say you think that must be very nice for the children,—and so it is, when, like these little folks, they do not choose very bad things; but I should not like to try that plan with any other but Japanese children, for I am sure there are no others who are naturally so good as they are.

But there are some very evil things in their life, and some of them come from that very want of government and care. They are a dirty, sore-eyed, sore-headed, crook-backed, miserable, and diseased-looking set of little creatures, and neither they nor their parents know of any better life. They throng about one every step one goes in the streets, and it takes a great deal of patience and pity to get along with them.

There is one thing that looks very strange. Almost every child one sees going about the streets, from six to ten or twelve years of age, seems, if coming towards you, to have two heads. Now, how do you suppose that can be? Well, I will tell you. The little children are all carried on the back, instead of in the arms, and so the larger children are made to carry the little babies strapped on their backs, as the easiest and safest way for them to take care of them; and as they come towards you, you can see only the head of the baby over the shoulder of the other child, and thus it seems as if it had two heads; and I have a good many times, until I became used to it, been quite startled by seeing such an odd sight.

It is a very hard way for the poor baby, though, for when it goes to sleep, as it very often does, its poor little head falls back, and the sun shines right down upon its face and eyes, and it looks as if its neck would break off.

None of the grown people or children ever wear hats, or anything to protect the head from the sun, except that the big people carry umbrellas, but the little folks do not. Almost all the children have dreadful sores about them. The people are very wicked, and have some very bad practices; and God punishes them by letting them be weak and sickly, and have these horrid diseases, and the poor little children have to suffer for it. It makes me so sorry for them, for they cannot help it, you know. And then, what makes it still worse, there are so many fleas and mosquitoes here, and you can guess how it hurts these little ones to have them get in the sores and bite them so badly.

The saddest thing to me is, that they

do not know any better life. The parents of these children do not know that if they would live pure, industrious, and proper lives, they would not have these dreadful diseases. They do not know that the idols they pray to cannot make them well, but that our God can do it.

I saw a boy one day, who had very sore eyes, go into a temple, which you know is their church, and go up to a great, hideous idol, or image, as high as the top of your room, all painted red and black and white, with its mouth wide open, and its tongue hanging out, and looking, O, so very ugly! and he began to rub his hands all over the feet and legs of the god, and then rubbed his own eyes.

I asked Mr. B—— what that was for, and he said that was the god that cured sore eyes, and the people came there to rub their hands first on the god, and then on their eyes, expecting to be cured.

Do you not think we ought to try and teach them better, and help them learn about our dear Father in heaven, and our kind, loving Saviour, who went about when He was in this world, healing all kinds of disease and sickness; and that He is just the same now, able and willing to do all that they desire, if they will only believe in Him, and pray to Him, instead of praying to their hideous wooden idols.

Another thing which makes me so sorry, and of which I believe I have told you before — *they never sing.*

It is so pleasant to hear our little folks at home sing their sweet and beautiful Sabbath school hymns; but these poor little ones have never been taught that they have voices that could be used for such a purpose. There is not one hymn written in their language. How much pleasure they lose! Do you not think so?

You know that we ladies in this house, and all the missionaries indeed, want to teach them these precious truths that make our own dear little folks at home so much wiser and happier than they are. Do you not think this is right? And will you not do all you can to help us?

A little black-and-white messenger came all the way across the big sea, and told me that Bertie had said, "Why can't grandma tell the heathen children about Jesus without my pennies?" Is that so, Bertie? Did you say just that? Well, so I could tell them; only you must remember they speak a different language from the one we use, and they could not understand me if I tried ever so hard to talk with them. Now, what would you do in such a case? I'll tell you what we want to do, and I guess you will think it the very best thing possible. We have a nice house, and it is all fixed up pleasant and comfortable. Now, we want to get a good many of these children to come here every day to school, and some we hope will come and live with us all the time.

The first thing we shall try to do, will be to teach them to talk as we do. Then we can tell them all about our dear Lord Jesus, and how they should love and serve Him. We can tell them then how wicked it is to pray to gods made of wood and stone, who cannot hear or help them. Now, you know it costs a great deal of money to buy a house, and get tables, and chairs, and beds, and dishes, and all those things that are needed to make a home comfortable. Then, too, they must have food every day, and a cook to get it ready for them to eat. Clothes, too, must be had, and some one to wash them, and to keep everything nice and clean in the house. Now, don't you know that for all these things your papa has to pay money? And it is just the same here in Japan, only some things cost more than they do in America.

So you see we must have money, and a good deal of it, too; and where shall we get it, if the dear friends at home do not send it to us? And we want the children's help, too, and Bertie's pennies are needed just as much as grandma's presence and voice.

My dear little children, who have such a happy and comfortable home, who have the precious Bible, and know so much of the love of our dear Father in heaven, I hope will pity these poor, ignorant ones, and desire to do something for them. I hope they will rather save their pennies, and put them in the Mission Box, than to spend them all for their own pleasure. That would be only selfish, and make your hearts grow hard and unkind; but if you try to do good, and help others all you can, you will grow more and more like the dear Saviour, and will surely be more happy and beloved by others. I will pray that God will make you all just such children.

Your loving

GRANDMA.

XI.

YOKOHAMA, July 26, 1872.

MY DEAR LITTLE FOLKS AT HOME:

I wanted to write a letter to each one
of my little folks to-day, but the time has
run away so fast that I find it quite im-
possible to do it, and so, as usual, I must
put it all together, and you can claim it
as your own. I have so much to tell you:
O dear! if I could only write faster! but
I can't, and you must just take what I
can do. Among all the pleasant things
that are coming to us these days, I will
only tell you of one which has made me
so happy that I want everybody to know
it, and to join me in praising God.

I want to tell you how God helped us

to "set up a family altar" for our servants. Do you know what that is? I think you do, and so I need not explain it to you; but you do not know what a wonderful thing it is to have some of these heathen people meet every day in one place, and listen to the reading of God's holy word, and then join in His worship. And you do not know, perhaps, this is the very first time, and the first house in which this has ever been attempted in this country, although it is more than two thousand years old. And this is what makes it so remarkable, and gives us such cause for joy.

There is one young man who became a Christian a short time ago. He was married a few weeks since, but he was so poor that he could not hire a house to live in. It was proposed to us to let him and his wife live in a little room which

we had attached to our school-house, and
he was asked, if we gave him this room,
if he would be willing to come in every
morning and read the Bible and pray with
our family in Japanese.

The people here are not allowed by
the government to do this; and if they are
detected in doing so, they can be taken
by the officers and put in prison. This is
the reason why none of the missionaries
have tried before to have family worship.
We thought, however, it was our duty to
make the trial, and somehow I felt very
sure it would please God, and He would
help us. So, when it was proposed to
Shonoski, — for that is the young man's
name, — he said he was not afraid to worship God, and he would do the best he
could.

And so he commenced, and now every
morning, after our prayers in English, I

go out on our piazza and ring the bell, and then Shonoski and his wife come from their little room, with their copy of the gospel of Mark, which is translated into Japanese; and from the other little houses and the kitchen our servants all gather so quickly and pleasantly, that any one can see that it is a delight and not a hard task: and then they have their prayers together; and once more the offering of praise and prayer goes up to our God. O how happy it makes me, and I sometimes weep for joy, as I see how eagerly these poor people listen to the words of life and truth!

I went down street this afternoon, and when I came home I found a dear little boy here, who had been brought by his mother to live with us. His father is a wicked Englishman, who has forsaken several little children, and cares not what becomes of them. The mother is a Japanese woman, and very poor; but she loves her children, and wants to have them taught to read English, though she is a heathen, and would rather not have them learn anything of our religion; for she thinks all Christians are like the father of her children, and if they get to be "Christein," they will be wicked as he is.

What is a little strange about this little fellow is, that although he had some other queer name before, his mother changed it to "Charlie," just to bring him here.

It is very common for these people to change their names whenever they please; but it seems so curious that she should choose the name that belonged to another one of my own dear children.

This little Charlie is a bright, handsome boy, just eight years old, and although he cannot speak a word of our language,

yet he seems to understand a good deal
that is said to him, and we all think we
shall love him very much.

Now we have Eddie, Annie, Minnie,
and Charlie — all *my own* names. Don't
you think it must seem a good deal like
home to me?

Good-by, and love, from

GRANDMA.

7

XII.

YOKOHAMA, Oct. 12, 1872.

MY DEAR BERTIE:

Some time ago I wrote part of the account of my visit across the bay. Now I think I must give all the little folks at home the rest of the story. I suppose you do not remember all I told you in that letter; but you must read it over, and then, by "putting this and that together," you will be able to understand it all.

The first night we spent at Sakuma's — for that was the name of our host — they thought they would be very kind, and give us beds; so they brought in some large wooden doors, and laid them up a

little above the floor, on some big blocks,
and then spread over them some red
woollen blankets. These were something
very nice, according to their ideas, for,
as wool has never been grown or used
in Japan, it is only very lately that they
have seen any kind of woollen goods.
Some foreign merchants have brought a
large number of blankets, of all colors,
and the Japanese think them wonderful.
Any person who is rich enough to buy
some of these is very proud to have
them, and so our friend was willing to
gratify his pride, and make us comfortable, as he thought, by letting us use his
new blankets.

We tried the beds, but we found them
very hard, notwithstanding the blankets,
and concluded the mats on the floor were
easier than the doors.

The next morning, when we began our

preparations for breakfast, the friends in the house arranged the doors for our table, and put the blankets on again *for the table-cloth.* This was decidedly disagreeable, but politeness required us to keep silent; and we ate at the "table," though we were very careful not to let any of the food lie upon it.

After breakfast we prepared to visit a mountain, about twelve miles distant, called Karnozan. This is a very celebrated place, both on account of the beautiful village and grand old temples right on the top of the mountain, and for the wonderful view there is from one particular spot, where we looked down upon ninety-nine valleys. All over among those valleys were scattered little villages and farms, which made the scene most charming.

We were caught in a grand thunder-

storm, and it was a sublime sight to see
the dark, angry-looking clouds rolling
among the hills below us, as well as
over our heads. I am never afraid of
the thunder, and can enjoy such a storm.
I believe I must stop here to tell you
why I am never afraid, and perhaps it
will help to keep you from fear.

When I was a very little girl, only five
years old, one Sabbath evening we were
sitting all together in the wide old hall,
saying our catechism, — which in those
days all the children were taught very
carefully, — when a terrific thunder-storm
came up. I was greatly frightened, and
began to cry, when my dear mother took
me up on her lap, and, as she sat rocking me in the old-fashioned chair in
which she was sitting, she taught me
these beautiful lines: —

"Jehovah sits upon the clouds,
 And governs all the sky;
He rolls the thunder round the globe,
 And bids the lightning fly."

Ever since that night I have always known that God is in the storm as well as in the sunshine, and I have often thanked Him that it is so sweet, and makes me feel so safe, to believe He is *my* Father, and able to take care of me in every place. Do you feel so? And are you glad to know that God is everywhere, and in all things?

And now we will come back to our story. The storm lasted so long that we were obliged to stay up on the mountain all night, for which I was not sorry, though we had neither bedding nor food of our kind there. Still we got along very well, and thought it paid us to bear some hardships for the privilege of seeing such a grand storm, and then witnessing a glorious sunrise in the morning.

That evening we returned to Sakuma's house, and, according to arrangements, Mr. B—— had a meeting of all the people on the place, to explain to them what the Christian religion is.

The large room, or hall, in which the people gathered, was a very strange-looking place. All the old houses in Japan become very black, and the reason is, they have a fashion of washing the wood-work with water in which they put lampblack or soot. After many years this makes the wood very smooth and shiny, and it looks exactly like that black wood they call ebony. The room in which we all met was like this, and as the Japanese never have many lights in the evening, and what they have are very dim,—only a small taper in a saucer of oil,—you must try

and imagine how dark and queer everything looked.

Just fancy a very large room, with nearly all the side walls, and all overhead,
jet black; a few small, dim lights scattered around on one side, and at one end
large altars, or shrines, on which there
were, probably, thirty of the household
idols, some very rich, and some small and
poor, but all worshipped by the family;—
imagine at one end of the room quite a
crowd, perhaps fifty or sixty dark-skinned,
bald-headed people (for the men all have
the tops of their heads shaved) sitting on
the floor; at the other end, Mr. B——,
the party with him, and the gentleman
of the house with his family,—and then
you will know how it looked in that meeting, which was the *first* ever held in that
part of the country where the name of
Christ was made known. O, it was de-

lightful to me to see all those people so
anxious to hear the gospel! They were
not willing to have Mr. B—— stop talking; and when he did, after ten o'clock,
they began to question Ogawa, and kept
him there with them till nearly twelve
o'clock.

Is it not hard to leave such people to
worship their dumb idols, just because
there is no one to go and live among
them, and teach them the truth!

This we had to do the next morning,
when we came away, and it made us all
sad, for they wanted so much to have
some one stay; but this, however, could
not be. But I will tell you what we all
resolved to do; and that is, pray that
God will bless the words that have been
spoken, and make them like good seed,
that may be hid for a while, but some
time will bear much fruit. We are going

to pray, too, that God will send more missionaries to Japan, so that there may be one to go to this place.

Will you help us by praying, too? You know I believe in children's prayers, and now that I have told you so much about this place and people, you will know just what to ask God for.

And now my long story is ended, and I will only say that I love you all as dearly as ever, and pray for you constantly.

GRANDMA.

XIII.

YOKOHAMA, Nov. 10, 1872.

MY DEAR LITTLE FOLKS AT HOME:

I suppose you have heard, through my letters to the big people, all about our moving into a nice, large house, and how happy we all feel, because now we can take more into our family, and be so much more comfortable: so I will not tell you anything more about that. But there is something in all our gladness that has made us feel very bad; it was one of the hardest things for me that has happened since I came to Japan. I know, you too will feel sorry when I tell you we have sent away from our home all the little boys who were with us.

You all know how I love the boys, and
you can imagine that little Charlie and
Eddie were especially dear to me, for
they seemed to come a little into the place
of those who were once " my very own; "
but we had found by trial that it was not
wise to have boys and girls together, unless they can have separate rooms at all
times. This we could not arrange; and
after talking a great deal over it, and praying for a long time that God would show
us the best way, we decided that, on a
certain day, their friends must come and
take them all away.

O, what a sad day it was! for the poor
little fellows did not want to go, and cried
so bitterly, that it made us ladies cry as
much as they. One little boy, when he
got outside the gate, threw himself down
on the grass beside the road, and said,

with pitiful sobbing, "I won't go; I *can't* go from this house."

It was only because we thought it was God's will, and we could do more good to the girls if we had them alone, that we could be firm, when we saw how grieved the poor little things were. But now we must all pray that God will provide some good friends for the boys, and give them a home just like this, where they can be taught about Jesus, and learn how they can grow up to be good Christian men.

After this, then, you must always think of this as a school and home for girls ; but I hope Bertie will not think that is any reason why he should not work for us, and save all his pennies, because the girls who are taught in this school are going to be teachers themselves by and by, and then they can help to instruct the boys, and so do a great deal more for them than we can.

I want now to tell you a little story about one of our dear girls — the little Annie of whom I have so often written.

I went to the breakfast-table one morning, as I generally do, to wait upon the children, and hear their Bible verses, which they always repeat at that time, when I found that Annie was not there. I asked why she was absent, and was told she was sick; so I went immediately to her room, but found, upon questioning her, that she only had a little stomach-ache, and was staying in bed, more because she felt (as little folks often do, you know) a little lazy and sleepy, and did not want to get up so early.

"O, come, come," said I; "we want you to get up, and come and eat your breakfast; and if you feel sick after that, you may go to bed again. Now hurry and dress, and come quickly."

Then I went back to the table; but very soon a gentleman called with a work-man, to see about repairing the ceilings that had been shaken down by a very hard earthquake. This gentleman was very kind, and wanted to help me; and so he had come to talk with the Japanese mason, and show him how to do the work. The ceiling in the room where Annie slept was one that was broken, and we had to go there to look at it. When we entered the room, there was the dear child on her knees beside her little bed, alone, saying her morning prayers. She did not jump up afraid, or hasten to finish, but, very quietly, with eyes closed, and her little hands clasped, she softly repeated her usual prayer. The gentleman, who is not a Christian, looked at her for a moment, and then, turning to me, as the tears gathered in his eyes, said, "That is very sweet."

I wonder how many little Christian children in America would have acted just as our Annie did. Do you not think *you* would have been in too great a hurry to get to the breakfast-table, when you knew the rest were almost finished, to stop for praying? Or do you not suppose you would have been startled by a stranger coming in, and would have jumped up off your knees?

I hope dear Annie's example will help you, my dear children, and that prayer for you, as for her, will be something so sweet, and so sacred, that nothing can hinder you in your devotions.

Ever your loving

GRANDMA.

XIV.

YOKOHAMA, March 12, 1873.

MY DEAR BERTIE:

It seems a long while since I wrote to any of the little folks at home, but I know you are all too kind and generous to feel vexed or cross about it. You hear from me very often through mamma's letters, and you know what a large family we are getting, and how much work I have to do nowadays.

. . . I don't think I have ever told you anything about the severe earthquakes we have in Japan. I think in this letter I must try and give you some little idea of these sources of terror and expense in this land.

This empire of Japan, although a comparatively small country, is composed of nearly four thousand islands, large and small, lying along the eastern coast of Asia, in the Pacific Ocean. It is only the four largest of these islands, however, that are generally included in what we call Japan. They are all very rough and irregular, and have no doubt been formed by being thrown up by terrible earthquakes.

There have been several volcanoes among these islands, that are now extinct, but there are yet some that send up their smoke and fire continually. All this proves that there are great internal fires, and it is, no doubt, because of these that the earthquakes are so constantly felt.

In our part of America, anything like an earthquake is very rarely known, and so you have never had any experience of them.

I don't suppose any description I can give will enable you to realize how strange and dreadful it is to have the house rocking over your head; the pictures on the walls swinging backward and forward; the timbers creaking and straining as if they must all come apart; to look out the window, and see the trees and bushes shaking from one side to the other All this, I think, we must see and feel ourselves, before we can know how dreadful it is; but sometimes even worse things happen.

That is what I want to tell you, and then you can see why it costs so much money to live here. Often these earthquakes shake the entire roof from a house; and the way it comes is this: The houses here are built very differently from American houses. They put a rough board covering on the top; over that they lay a thick coat of soft, black mud, and then, in the mud, they lay the hard, stone tiles, that you will see in the pictures, and which make the roofs look so pretty. After some time the mud gets very dry, and becomes just like dust, and then if an earthquake comes and shakes the house hard, the whole roof will slide right off down upon the ground.

Not only this, but often the chimneys tumble down, and the plaster falls off the sides of the house; the fences are thrown down, and in many ways a great deal of damage is done. Sometimes we cannot help feeling a little discouraged. We get the masons and carpenters to work, and, with a great deal of trouble, we succeed in getting every thing all nicely repaired, and then, perhaps, in two or three days, another storm or earthquake will come, and undo all our work again.

Yet we try to be patient. We always feel so thankful, after it is over, that no person has been hurt; and it gives us occasion to prove our trust in God. David said in one of his sweet psalms, " Therefore will not we fear, though the earth be removed, and though the mountains be carried into the midst of the sea; " and it is always very sweet for me to repeat those words, and to feel that God is *our* refuge.

One night we were all quietly sleeping, when there came one of the severest shocks I have ever felt. Our children are so used to them that they do not often get frightened; but it was very startling to be fairly shaken out of a sound sleep, and some of them began to scream and run wildly about; this frightened others, and soon there was a terrible commotion.

We always keep a hanging light burning in the hall, and in a moment or two every woman and child was gathered there.

We took the poor little scared creatures in our arms, and, hushing their fears as well as we could, we tried to tell them of the loving care of the great God who can take up in His hand all these thousands of islands "as a very little thing," and yet never forgets even one of His little helpless children.

How sweet it is to trust in Him, and to *know* that we are always safe in His hands! . . .

Ever your loving

GRANDMA.

XV.

YOKOHAMA, April 20, 1873.

DEAR MARY:

I know you will let Bertie and Kittie feel that this letter is partly theirs; but sometimes I like to send one just directed to one of you, so that you can feel more as if I was thinking of, and talking to you all by yourself. And then it gives you the opportunity to be generous, and let others share your happiness.

I want you to learn this while you are young, and as you grow older you will find there is no pleasure so great as that we enjoy in making others happy. Those people who are selfish, and always trying to study what will please and gratify themselves, are very far from being the happiest persons; and if you will take grandma's experience and advice as your rule, you will always try to put yourself last, and seek to please others first. But I am not going to preach a sermon to you, and I will now do what I first commenced this letter for, and that is, tell you about a picnic our little folks had on our beautiful lawn.

You know we have very large grounds about this new house, and at the back of it,—which is really not at all like the back of a house, only we have to call it so,— there is a large, circular plot of grass. Around this is a wide gravelled road for carriages, that can come in the large gate, and drive close up to the back door.

Then, outside of the carriage-road are large beds, filled with all kinds of beautiful shrubs and evergreen trees, with

some flowers. Among these, too, there
are piled up, as only the Japanese know
how to do, common, rough stones, that are
covered with beautiful little vines and
plants, growing out of the crevices, filled
with earth. Some of these are very curi-
ously arranged, and all look so pretty
among the trees and bushes, that I often
wish the gardeners in America knew how
to use rough stones as the Japanese do.

All this makes a very pleasant place to
play, and our children do not need to go
away from home for pleasure; but as we
like to do all we can to make them happy,
we thought we would give them a tea-
party out on the lawn, and let them have
a good frolic among the trees.

We had a great tall bamboo pole set
up in the middle of the grass circle, and
by cords and pulleys raised our beautiful
flag, with its stars and stripes, to the top

of it, and when it floated out in the breeze, we almost felt like teaching the girls to "hurrah," as the boys do; for we never can look upon our own flag without longing to hear some one shout. Around the flag-pole we had beautiful twigs and bushes twined for some distance from the ground, and then some pretty little evergreens set out all about it, so that it looked as if it stood in a miniature forest.

Then we set a long table at one side, and on it we had all the flowers, vines, and wreaths that we could get or con-trive. We had bread, with nice jam spread on it (the Japanese never eat butter), crackers, cakes of many kinds, oranges, nuts, and a good many varieties of candy, which the native bakers make. These candies are very harmless and very cheap, yet very pretty. They do not have much sugar in them, but are made nearly all of millet and rice-flour. I never saw any table look prettier than ours did, and we were all so glad, for you see the Japanese people never sit at a table when they eat, and none of our girls had ever seen a large table so prettily ornamented before. We want them to know how nice it is to live like civilized people, and so we are trying in this way to show them.

The children were all dressed in their best clothes, and although all their dresses are dark, mostly blue, yet they generally wear a bright *obi*, or sash, and something bright fastened in their hair. This makes them look quite pretty, and when they were all together, out on the lawn, play-ing pretty games, we ladies thought it was as beautiful a sight as we could desire, although there were no rich and elegant garments among them.

They had all sorts of plays, and if I

had time, I would like to describe some of them, they are so queer; but I cannot do it now. After playing, and singing, and doing just as they pleased for a long time, we directed them to sit down right on the grass, in a half circle, around the table, and then the ladies helped them to all the good things. And it was very pleasant to see how quiet and polite they were; no haste, no selfishness, no fault-finding, as I have sometimes seen among the children in America, at picnics or parties, but all so happy, and careful to do exactly as they were told.

When the tea was over, they had a merry chase around the flag-pole, another game or two, some singing, and then the picnic was over, and the little ones went to bed, and the larger girls to the study-room, to get their lessons for the next day.

Now, don't you think the children here have a good time, and are you not glad grandma is here to help make them happy? I am sure you are; and now I can only say, I hope our dear Father in heaven will give you, and each one of my dear children, many happy and useful days.

Your affectionate

GRANDMA.

XVI.

SHIDZOOKA, May 9, 1873.

MY DEAR CHILDREN:

As you will see from this date, I am writing from a new place. This is Mr. C——'s home; and as I am a sort of mother to him now, I came here to see how nice he lives, and enjoy the pleasure of travelling in Japan. Well, pleasure it is; though if I could tell you all the discomforts by the way, you would wonder how I could say so; but I am so desirous of seeing the country, and getting acquainted with all the customs and habits of the people, that I am quite willing to bear some inconveniences.

I have written a very long letter about

this old city, and my experiences in getting here, and I suppose you little folks will hear papa or mamma read that; but I am going to tell you just two things that have happened since I came, which I think it will please you to read about.

The first is a visit to an old temple, and the ride in going and coming away. Mr. C—— is occupied every day in his school, and so he asked a young Japanese gentleman to go with me, and show me the very large temple which is one of the great objects of interest in this great city.

I ought to tell you first, however, that Shidzooka is a very large city, about one hundred miles south of Yokohama, and is celebrated because it was the home of the first Tycoon, who built here a grand castle, with three great moats, or canals, around it. The castle is now all in ruins;

a great heap of immense stones, with vines and bushes growing all over them.

Mr. C——'s house is built on one corner of the outermost wall of the moat, and from it I can look in one direction far off over the city; in the other, over the successive moats and intervening grounds, I see those wild and grand old ruins.

But about the temple. We started in our *jin-ri-ki-sha;* but no sooner were we outside of the wall of the moat, than the people began to see that some strange being was among them; for you must know I was the first foreign lady who had ever been in that city.

They tried to run after us, men, women, and children, the crowd getting larger and larger every moment. Our coolies seemed to understand that this was very disagreeable to me, and tried to go very fast, and through back streets, but it did

RIDING IN A JIN·RI·KI·SHA.

(From a Photograph.)

not prevent their following, though we reached the temple, and got inside the gate a little ahead.

I wish I could tell you all about the temple, which is remarkable for its immense size and great number of apartments, but I have not time. After we had gone all over it, we went towards the front porch, when I heard such a noise, talking, and shouting, and the clattering of wooden clogs upon the stone pavement of the court, that I could not summon courage to go out there. I asked the gentleman if there was not a back door; but, after going away to inquire, he told me this was the only way, and so I was obliged to go out.

O, what a sea of faces appeared before me as I stepped upon that porch, and every one so curious, so noisy, and for aught I could tell, so angry; for you know

all over this country there are a great
many who hate foreigners, and are not
willing to let them travel among them. I
could see, too, that the gentleman who
was with me was getting very nervous,
and, indeed, it required a good deal of
courage for him to conduct me about
under all the circumstances. Beyond the
noise, and crowding close to get a good
look at me, taking hold of my garments,
and even catching at my hands, to see, I
suppose, if I was really flesh and blood,
there was nothing to excite fear, or that
showed any unkindness.

We got safely into the *jin-ri-ki-sha*,
and once more started through the streets,
the same crowd running as hard as they
could to keep up with the coolies. On
the way back, I wanted to call and see
the father and mother of one of the young
Christian men in Yokohama, who had very

earnestly desired me to do so. They were
delighted to see me when they found I
knew their son so well; and when I expressed, as mere politeness, my admira-
tion of a beautiful rose-tree, which was
growing beside the door, the father ran
away, and in a moment came back with
a large knife, and before I could imagine
what he was going to do, he cut it right
off close to the ground, and, with its great
clusters of magnificent flowers, presented
it to me, with a most profound bow.
When I tell you that roses are just beginning to be cultivated in Japan, and the
people prize them very highly, you will
understand what an expression of politeness and pleasure this was.

What to do with the great bush I did
not know; but finally asked Mr. H——— if
he could take it in his *jin-ri-ki-sha*. Upon
this, the gentleman of the house ran away

again, and came back with a strong cord;
with this he tied the rose-bush upon the
top of the *jin-ri-ki-sha*, so that it formed
a beautiful canopy over his head.

Then we started for home; but the
flowers made Mr. H——'s *jin-ri-ki-sha*
even more an object of attraction than I
was, and the poor fellow was so com-
pletely worried, or scared, I do not exactly
know which, by all the excitement and
commotion of our excursion, that when
we reached our home he was as pale as
a ghost, and for two or three days was
really quite unwell.

Another event occurred the other evening, that I want to tell you about. That
was a musical party, which was gotten up
by some of Mr. C——'s Japanese friends,
to let us hear something of their kind of
music. I have told you, in other letters,
that the Japanese never sing. Well, this

is true of what we call singing; yet they have some rude and queer musical instruments, and practise a strange kind of low, monotonous humming, which they call singing, but which really has not the first idea of true music in it. The men who performed on the instruments showed considerable skill, and it was a great gratification to me to see their ancient and curious mode of performance.

I was more interested, however, in the part of the entertainment which showed how the ladies of the higher classes in Japan are educated, and what their ideas of musical performances are.

There were five ladies; one the wife of one of Mr. C——'s interpreters, a bright, sprightly little thing, not more than fifteen or sixteen years old, and the others all plain, middle-aged women.

I wish I could picture the group, as they

sat upon the floor in a half circle; one
with a *koto*, a long, flat instrument, with
strings like a harp; two of them with a
samisen, very like a banjo, the other two
to do the singing, or humming, as I should
call it. The little wife would have been
very pretty, with her bright eyes, red
cheeks, and rich, fanciful dress; but she
had black teeth, colored, as all the married
women must do, with some unfortunate
preparation, and this made her look to me
very disagreeable and ugly. They played
and sang a great many different pieces,
but they seemed very nearly alike to me,
and I was more gratified by the opportunity to see and hear what was so novel
to me, than with the performance itself.

After the singing, the little wife danced
one of the strange dances of Japan. I
cannot attempt to describe it, it was so
singular and curious. It was intended to

express, by acting, the history of a battle, a love story, and a death.

Altogether, my visit in Shidzooka was one of very great pleasure and interest to me, and if you want to know more, you must get some one to read my letters to the big folks.

And now I must once more bid you good-by, and ask our dear Father to take good care of all my precious ones "over the sea."

Always, with warmest love,

GRANDMA.

XVII.

YOKOHAMA, May 16, 1873.

MY DEAR YOUNG FRIENDS:

I wonder if the "little ones" in the dear home-land, who, with loving hearts and nimble fingers, did so much towards filling the boxes that came to this "Island of the Sea," would not like to hear something about "the children's table" in our Bazaar. I am sure they will be very glad and thankful to know that all their gifts came to us safely, and that it did us "good like a medicine," to see so many pretty and useful things that we knew were made by little fingers. I took a great deal of pains to show them to all the little girls in our Home, and to have them understand that the children in far-off America had been saving up their money, and spending their time to prepare all those gifts, because they loved *them*, and wanted to help to keep them in this pleasant Home, where they are taught of Jesus and his love.

We gathered all the articles we fancied had been made by little fingers, and placed them in the middle of one of the long tables of our "Bazaar." How pretty was the sight of so many beautiful dolls, and their clothes, and their little bedsteads, and all the things children love so well! Then we told our little girls we would let them sell the pretty things, and how pleased and happy that made them, you can hardly imagine. As we have so many children, we arranged that they should take turns in selling, and placed some of the smallest on chairs near the larger ones.

Dear Miss Guthrie had a busy time in directing all of them, and seeing that they were all dressed in their very best clothes; for you see, we wanted our children to look as well, when they were going to see strangers, as the dear mothers at home do.

Sometimes it would be Minnie, Sono, Fannie, and Annie; then, Sake, Bessie, Mary, Hanna, and Nina, would take their turn; then, perhaps, there would be Jennie and Ilo, and Kai and Haru, or little Mabel and Mamie, and Kiku, Maggie, Yasu, Sie, would come; and so, for the three days of our Bazaar, each afternoon our dear children had just the happiest time you can think of.

I believe it made the ladies who came to purchase think more about our Home and school. I feel quite sure, if we have another sale like that, they will be more glad to help us than they were before; for now they know just how happy it is for little children to be here, rather than in their dark heathen homes. So you see, my dear young friends, you have not only helped us to get some money to build more rooms, so that we can receive into our " Home " all who desire to come here, but you have also given to our little ones three of the brightest days they have ever known.

May the dear Saviour bless each one of you, and help you to send up to Him earnest prayers that all our dear family may become His own children.

Ever your loving friend,

M. P.

XVIII.

YOKOHAMA, July 10, 1873.

MY DEAR ONES AT HOME:

Once more grandma sits down, with her pen in hand, to write to her dear little children in the precious home in Pearl Street. This Home is very dear to me, and I am very happy, as I see around me so many dear children, and sweet, gentle young girls, and know that they are learning those truths and those customs that must surely make them wiser and happier than they could be in their heathen homes; but still my heart goes far over the sea very often, and it is a real comfort when I can sit down and have a little talk with the children there.

I have a very sweet little story for you to-day, and I know you will be glad to read it, for it shows you how God is making this a real Christian home for the dear children who come to it.

One dear little girl in our " Home," who united with the foreign church, has been developing quickly and sweetly in her Christian character. For a long time I have been in the habit of giving the children a short text to learn each day, and repeat at the breakfast-table. Minnie sleeps in a room adjoining mine, and always hears the little ones say their morning prayers. I used to hear them talking and repeating their verses, and did not notice anything special. One morning, in passing through that room, I found it quite full, and the children all seated in their chairs in so orderly a way, that I made some remark commending them; when

Minnie said, "I had a good many at my meeting; there were fourteen here." "Your meeting!" I replied; "do you have a meeting?" "O, yes," she answered; "I have had one for more than a week, and they are all beginning to like to come." And so, in this quiet, unostentatious way, she was gathering these dear children each morning, for "a little talk with Jesus." Was it not sweet, and do you not quite agree with me that the dear Lord Jesus sent that child to be a comfort and help to us?

With love to you all,

GRANDMA.

XIX.

YOKOHAMA, January 4, 1874.

DEAR CHILDREN:

While everything connected with our pleasant Christmas is fresh in my mind, I want to have a chat with the kind friends, especially the "little ones" who sent all the pretty things for our bazaar a year ago. I suppose it seems a long time to them, and perhaps they thought they would never hear any more of their work. Yet I have a good deal to tell them of the happiness their gifts conferred upon the dear children and young girls in our school at Christmas eve. When we began to talk about a Christmas-tree this year, we were quite at a loss to know what to do. You

see we had no one at home who had
promised to send a box of articles for such
a purpose, as they do for the children in
India. Many of the sailors who helped us
last year had gone away, and several rea-
sons prevented our asking assistance from
the people here; so we hardly knew how
we could have a tree. The school has
grown so much that it was quite impossi-
ble for the ladies of our family to assume
the expense. All at once it occurred to
me that there were some boxes filled with
articles that were left after the bazaar,
which we had very carefully put away,
hoping some time to receive more goods,
and have another sale. So we talked about
it, and came to the conclusion that those
who sent the articles would like to have
such as were suitable for gifts used for
that purpose. In looking over the things,
we were surprised and delighted to find

how many were appropriate, in fact, seemed as if they were made for the purpose. Now our dear children could have such a nice tree and a " Merry Christmas " like the little people in America.

There were many wise and curious looks from the little ones. Many little heads were peering around every time the door of a certain room was opened, and many surmises, if a piece of wrapping-paper or a bundle was seen. You see that little Japanese girls are exactly like our American children in such things, and although they were never obtrusive or selfish, yet they were very curious.

Miss Crosby agreed to adorn the school-room, and asked a number of girls to arrange greens in wreaths, and sew them on pasteboard letters. That, you know, is a good deal of work; it kept them very busy; but how well they did it! A number of persons said they had never seen so pretty a room.

But I have been going too fast. I must go back and tell you what a merry time some of the girls and younger children had, "popping" corn and stringing it for the tree. It was great fun for them, for many of them had never seen such a thing before. The best of that "pop-corn" to me was, that it grew on our own farm. General Capron gave me some seed, and I, thinking all the time of the pleasure it would give, had a good deal planted, and now we have enjoyed it just as I knew we would. Then we made large bags of mosquito-netting, and filled them with pop-corn and Japanese candy, and hung them on the tree, one for every child.

At last the tree was all ready, and I am very sure if our dear friends at home could have seen the happy faces that filled the

room as the gifts were all distributed, with
the cakes and fruits we provided, they
would not only have been glad that so
many things were left from the bazaar, but
they would have said, "I mean to try and
help in providing a tree next year."   And
this is just what we want you to do; for
unless some one helps us, we cannot have
these pleasures.   I will tell you how one
little girl helped us.   She lives in Albany,
and often sends me letters and gifts.   But
at last she had a Fair in her papa's garden, and her little brother and sister
helped her, and they not only had a pleasant time, but she raised sixteen dollars,
which she sent me "to use for the children."

Your loving friend,

M. PRUYN.

XX.

YOKOHAMA, February 18, 1874.

MY DEAR CHILDREN:

Once more Grandma has a story to tell her little children "at home." How she does love to talk with them, and how nice it is to sit down here at this pretty desk, and say things on paper that will go all the way across the great ocean, and be read by the dear ones there. The only thing that is not pleasant is, that all "the talk" must be on one side. I cannot hear your voices, telling me what you think, and how you are spending your time. But sometimes when I get your letters, and read your "talk" to Grandma, I feel paid richly for those I send to you.

And now to my story. It is about one of our little girls, and I am going to let you guess which one it is; and I don't think it will be hard to do that, for I have written a good many times about her.

She has a father who came from Scotland, and drinks very hard. The doctor said he feared he would die soon if he did not stop, so I have tried to get him to make a will, and provide for his little girl after he is dead; but he does not believe he is in any danger, and has not yet done anything for her.

He has plenty of money now, but if he dies without a will, his little girl cannot have any of it, for her mother is a Japanese: and then she will be a poor child, and have to be supported by charity.

He wanted to have his little daughter come and see him last month, when he was very sick, and I could not refuse, though I did not like to have her stay even one night with such a bad father.

After she came home, I did not hear anything from him for about two weeks. Then I saw the doctor, and inquired about him, and asked the doctor if he would not try and get him to make a will, so that his little girl would not be left penniless.

The doctor promised to do what he could, but he said, "I do not think Mr. —— is going to die now. He has stopped drinking, and there seems to be a great change in him."

I was very glad to hear this, but did not know how to account for it till a day or two ago. The dear child was getting ready to go again to see him, and while waiting for something, she began to sing, "There is a happy land." I said, "When you are with your papa, you must sing that for him, and ask him if he wants to go to that 'happy land.'"

"Yes," she said; "and I'll tell him he must love Jesus, or he can't go." And then, after a moment, she said, " Last time, when I went to my papa's house, I told him he must pray to Jesus, and he said he would."

"Did you sing for him?" I asked.

"O yes," she said, "I sing and I pray, and I make my papa pray too."

Can this not be the secret of the change the doctor spoke of? I thought. Is not the influence of this dear child the cord by which God is lifting this ungodly father up to a purer and better life? I do hope it may prove so, and we will all rejoice and praise God.

I have just had a petition brought to me; and what do you think it was? As I was sitting writing, a soft knock was heard, and when I said, Come, the door was opened, and five little faces peeped in,

all full of fun and glee; and one said,
" Mrs. Pruyn, can't we play tea-party this
afternoon?" Now, I suppose you know
that tea-party means little dishes, cakes,
and nuts, and all the good things that
" mother" can find for the little ones. I
did want so much to be quiet, and write
this afternoon, but I could not resist all
these dear little faces; and so the dishes
were taken out, the Japanese tables and
bamboo stools were carried among the
bushes on the other side of the lawn, and
some crackers, grapes, and chestnuts were
put on little waiters; and now there are
sixteen as happy children as one could
ever see, playing out in that pleasant
place.

But all this has taken the time I meant
for you, and so I must close my letter,
with love to all from

GRANDMOTHER.

XXI.

YOKOHAMA, March 18, 1874.

To THE DEAR TEACHERS AND SCHOLARS OF
THE INDUSTRIAL SCHOOLS OF ALBANY:

I did not need the contribution of your
"mite boxes" to assure me of your kind
remembrance of me and my work, but it
awakened my gratitude, and prompts me
to tell you some of the blessings our
dear Lord Jesus sends to us in these far
away "Islands of the Sea."

I could not tell you all the Lord is doing for us, for His mercies are more than
can be numbered; nor will I write at this
time about our Home, and Day School,
for you have already heard considerable
of them; but I know you will be glad to

learn that away off here in Japan we have a real live Sabbath school, and of that I want to write now.

The history of this people goes away back a good many hundred years before Christ was born, so that when He came to this world, they were already an old nation; and yet do you know that the children in Japan have never heard of the dear Saviour, who, when he was on earth, showed such love for little children!

Even since the Christian missionaries came here, and taught a few of the large people the precious truths of the Bible, the children did not seem to be reached.

Well, you know our Home was opened especially for them, and so we feel that in every way possible we must try and do good to the children.

And thus it was that we decided to commence a Sabbath school, *the first one* ever opened in Japan.

For although there are a number of persons now teaching in various places and ways, and there are some classes of young men who meet for Bible study on the Sabbath, yet ours is the only real Sabbath school in the country that is conducted just as those are in America, which are so very pleasant and useful.

If you were to make us a visit, you would find, if you wished to see the opening of the school, you must be here promptly at half past three in the afternoon. The Japanese know nothing of the value of time, and punctuality is one of the hardest things for them to learn; so that we are very particular in counting the moments in all our dealings with them.

You would see a large, bright, cheery room, filled with little chairs and stools, for we do not let our children or their friends sit upon the floor, as they do in their own houses or temples; the desks which are used during the week are all set back against the wall, and only the middle of the room is occupied with seats.

There is a platform at one end, and on it a table with a Bible, hymn-book, and bell, and also a couple of large straw chairs. By the side of the platform stands a small organ, that would seem a very poor one, I suppose, in Albany, but it serves our purpose very well till we can get a better one.

About forty come together now, but the number increases so fast that, by the time you read this, there may be a great many more. Some are quite small, and others quite grown-up persons. They all sit together till after the opening exercises, which are very much like those in the Sunday schools at home. Then the classes form, and the smallest scholars go into another room with their teacher. This is our infant department; and a nicer, more properly behaved, and bright little company you could not find anywhere.

There are only three classes in the large room, each sitting in a circle around the teacher; but if you could see the eager, pleasant faces of the scholars turned towards that teacher, and hear the intelligent questions asked and answered by them, you would think the hour spent there a delightful one for both teachers and scholars.

When the hour is ended, no one seems tired, or in a hurry to get away; but punctuality is our rule; and then we like to have them hungry when they stop studying the Bible, for if so, they will be more likely to come the next Sunday.

Our closing exercises always seem very pleasant, and often we have visitors come

in, who express a great deal of satisfaction
and interest. Each class and each scholar
repeats a text that has been given them
the Sabbath before; a hymn is sung; the
Creed is repeated by the school, standing,
and the Lord's Prayer, all kneeling. I
should say that before these exercises
commence, the little children take their
places again in the large room.

Thus closes our Sabbath school at five
o'clock, and I am sure every teacher and
scholar feels that it has been a privilege
and pleasure to have been there.

And now, dear children, I thank you
most heartily for the pennies you saved
and sent to me. I know you have very
few, and I think the dear Lord will value
your gifts more highly than those from
children who have rich fathers and mothers, and plenty of good things.

I do desire that your faith and prayers

may be constantly brought to God, as a precious and acceptable offering for this cause. No money of yours, no labor of ours, will be of any value without the blessing of the Holy Spirit's power to accompany both; and I rejoice to believe that prayer is made for us by so many at home. I see in the wonderful blessings that have come upon this work the answers to those prayers, and I praise God for the dear, loving Christian friends in America, and especially in my own city, who so constantly bear us upon their hearts before the Mercy-seat.

That all your loving deeds and prayerful sympathy may return in rich and abiding blessings upon your own hearts and schools, is the fervent prayer of

Your ever affectionate friend,

MARY PRUYN.

11

XXII.

YOKOHAMA, August 20, 1874.

MY DEAR LITTLE ONES:

After a long absence from this home, I am once more seated at my little desk to write to you, my dear children in the home far over the sea. It is a pleasure to hear that you love to read my letters, and it makes me more desirous to tell you all I can about this beautiful country and these people, whom I am learning to love so much.

The place I have been visiting now is one of the most lovely and celebrated in Japan. It is the village of Hakone, far up on the mountains, which have the same name, and on the shore of a most charming lake. It is about forty miles from Yokohama, and being so high, is very cool and delightful in the hot season. For this reason many foreign people go up there in the summer time, to get away from the great heat of the cities.

The people are glad to rent their houses to the visitors, for they are very poor, and it is hard to make a living up there. I wish I could describe one of the houses to you, for one is a type of all.

The outside is not at all pretty — a low, dark-looking building, with a heavy thatched roof projecting over the front. As you go in, you see all the work of cooking, washing, &c. going on. You pass through a long, dark apartment, very large and very gloomy, where the family live during the daytime.

But, coming out at the back part of the house, you find it very different. Here are pleasant and beautifully clean apartments, which can be made large or small, just as one desires, by means of sliding paper doors. A narrow veranda runs across the back part of the house, and this is the usual sitting-place for the foreigners, who hire these houses to live in while they stay up on the mountains.

It is very pretty and comfortable when you get past the kitchen part, and look out upon the picturesque garden, which almost every Japanese house has behind it. Our mountain home had one that was very small, but it was large enough to have a lake, several little islands, some rustic bridges, two or three waterfalls, with shrubs and trees trained in many fantastic ways; and all this in a space not more than thirty feet square.

The Japanese do these things most perfectly, and the smaller the scale, the more beautiful everything seems.

The Lake of Hakone is like a diamond with the richest emerald setting. A lovely sheet of water, with grand old mountains rising all around it, covered with thick, rich grass and evergreens.

There are many places up there that I would like to tell you about. The fine old temples away up on the sides of the mountains; the immense stone images along the shores of the lake; the wild and desolate region called O'Jin-Oku, or the "Great Hell," because it is literally a place of "fire and brimstone," the smoke coming out in small jets all over the place, and the boiling-hot sulphur water pouring out of the rocks in many places, while the noise made by the roaring of the internal fires is equal to a steam-engine. I would tell you, too, of the grand view we had of the sacred mountain Fusiyama, when we clambered up to the top of one of the lesser mountains on the shore of the lake; but all this I must pass over, for I want to tell you of something that will show you what darkness these people are in, although they have so much about them that ought to teach them of the true God.

One day I was sitting in the back part of my house, when I heard a great noise, and saw the people in the kitchen all running to the street.

I went out to see what was the matter, and found a great crowd gathered right in front of the door. At first I could not tell what it meant; but pretty soon I saw that there was a "god's carriage" standing upon the ground, and a great company of men dancing around it.

The god from one of the large temples was being carried about for a ride, and the people on such occasions are very glad to have him stop near their houses,

for they think it will bring a blessing.
The man that kept our house, I think, had
invited them to rest there, and offered to
give *saki* to those who were carrying the
god. And so they stopped to drink, and
dance, and shout, just like so many
demons.

As I looked at the wretched creatures,
I could hardly think they were men. It
was the most dreadful exhibition of heathen
idolatry I have ever seen; and O, how it
made my heart ache for the poor, ignorant
creatures that can call that worship!

But there is a bright side to my visit up
on those beautiful mountains; and so I
must tell you that the true light of the
gospel is beginning to shine up there.

We had meetings for the women in our
rooms every day and evening, and Mrs.
P——, with two of our dear Christian girls,
told to all the people who came the " sweet

story of old," and sang many of our precious Sunday-school hymns for them.

Then our good Tokiche, who came with me and two other young Christian men, had meetings in a room, in another part of the village, and a great many men went there every night to hear the gospel preached. After a while, too, Mr. B—— came up there, and as he can talk their language well, he was able to teach them very plainly.

We are all thankful that God made the people willing to listen to the truth, and we know that a few have put away their idols, and are determined to worship the true God. We hope and pray that soon all the people will do this, for God has promised in His word that He will give Japan to Jesus for His possession. Do not cease to pray for this, my dear children, and also for

Your loving   GRANDMA.

XXIII.

AMERICAN MISSION HOME,
YOKOHAMA, January 18, 1875.

TO THE SUNDAY SCHOOL CHILDREN IN
AMERICA:

My dear young friends, an utter stranger
to you, I still feel that it is my privilege to
assume that we are friends; and so I am
going to write you a good long letter, and
tell you something about this Home, and
the work connected with it, in far-off
Japan.

I have no greater pleasure than to put
myself into communication with the dear
Sunday-school children in America. I
want them to be helpers with me in this
blessed work. The only unpleasant feeling I have in commencing this correspon-

dence, is the certainty that I cannot, by any written words, give you a just idea of the interesting and encouraging features of this work, or put before you as distinctly as I would like, the happiness of having a part in it. God has been so very good to us in this Mission Home, and has given us so soon to see many of our dear children taught to love and pray to Jesus, and it is such a real delight to all the ladies who are living in the house to have these dear young girls and little children right here in our own Home, and day by day to see them so well, so comfortable, so happy, that it always seems as though no one could understand it all, unless they could come here and see for themselves.

But this I know you cannot do; and I want to help you, if I can, to get acquainted with us, so that you may feel it a pleasure also to do what you can to support this Home. God could do all this work without money, and He could make these Japanese people good and happy Christians through the labors of other persons than the people and children of America; but I think He has been very kind and condescending, that He has chosen to give us the privilege, and that He will be pleased to use the money which even a little child may send from our Sunday schools, to convert and bless the Japanese. And the reason why I think this, is, because there is no country in the world where it is so pleasant to live and work for Jesus, and there are no people in the world who desire so earnestly to learn about Jesus. This seems to be the case with all classes; young and old, rich and poor, are all equally ready to listen, and willing to be convinced. So you see that those who work for, and who work in

Japan, have every reason to expect their work to prosper, and to feel that God is specially good to them in giving them such pleasant work to do.

I shall put in this letter a picture* which I want you all to look at carefully, and then you will know just how the outside of our school looks, and you will be better able to fancy all the bright, happy faces that. fill it day by day. There are only a few figures in the photograph, for we could not very well get all our family in; but there are enough to show you how these children and young ladies look, and enable you to judge how very good God has been in giving us such a nice school-house and such a pleasant home.

The school is the first and only free school ever built for the education of Japanese girls, though another one is just

* See frontispiece.

now commenced; and you will not wonder that we feel very desirous that it shall
be well sustained, prove a great blessing
in this land, and be an honor and cause
for praise to the Christian people of
America, through whose instrumentality
it was established. The large room, of
which you see the side, is the school-room
proper, and in it not only our school as-
sembles, but all the services of the native
Christian church are held, except one
preaching service on Sabbath morning,
which is held at another place. Here,
too, our dear Christian girls hold their
precious prayer-meetings; and our family
worship on Sunday morning — which is
really quite a little service, with an audi-
ence, when all our household are assembled, of over sixty souls — is also observed
in this room. The other room — the wing

on the rear — is used for the sewing and
writing department.

If I had time, I would like to show you
something of the inside of our dwelling-
house, especially the girls' study-room,
when they are all seated around the two
large tables in the evening, with their
books, so eager to learn that it is never
necessary to urge their attention, but rather to check them, and watch that they
do not neglect the proper recreation. I
would like to have you go into our nice,
new dining-room, that I particularly delight in, and see thirty-six girls and children — who only a short while ago were
accustomed to sitting upon the floor, and
any time, without order or idea of propri-
ety, eating what would satisfy their hun-
ger with chop-sticks or their fingers — now
sitting quietly and decorously around the
tables, with table-cloths, napkins, knives

and forks, eating their food as properly as any polite and neat American child could. Then I would love to take you in the little children's play-room, and let you see as merry and bright a little company as could be found anywhere, enjoying the gifts that kind friends in far-off America sent, and which found their way to a Christmas-tree a few weeks ago, and were from it distributed among our little folks; or I would go with you into the sleeping-rooms, and show you — particularly in one room — a row of little beds, and a row of little heads so cunningly nestled in the pillows that I never can pass them without stopping to kiss, and to breathe the prayer, "Dear Jesus, bless our little ones."

But all this, dear friends, you must try to imagine, and then consider whether you will not help us in this work of educating and converting from heathenism to the religion of Jesus the young people of Japan.

I must enclose in this letter still another picture, a photograph, of some of our Jap-

JAPANESE YOUNG LADIES.
(From a Photograph.)

anese young ladies, because I think you will be interested in seeing how they look.

I have not told you of what is more

precious to me, and I trust will be to you, than any temporal blessing or prosperity, and that is of the real love for Jesus that many of our dear family prove in their daily life. Yet I think that I must leave that also, and in some future letter give you some account of the fruits of this Christian life, particularly of the work some of our Christian girls are doing in visiting, reading the Bible, and praying among their people.

Just now I must tell you something that has pleased us all very much, concerning a little girl supported by a kind lady in America. I am sure you will all be especially glad to hear that O'Sono is such a bright and good girl, and that we have the greatest pleasure in witnessing her rapid improvement, and her quick, bright, and happy manners.

About two weeks ago, she went to visit

her mother. Her father, who had been a rich nobleman, had become very poor; but that does not change the character or position of people here, and he was just as much respected as though he had plenty of money. When the war commenced with Formosa, he got a good appointment, and went with the army to that country, but in a few weeks died of fever there. And so the poor mother was left alone, and now bitterly disappointed in her hope of some support for her family. When O'Sono was at home, General Saigo, who was the commander of the army in Formosa, and a great friend of her father, sent for O'Sono to come to his house and visit him with her mother. While she was there, he examined her in her studies, and after a great many questions, and hearing her read and sing, he expressed himself quite delighted, and said he had never heard any native pronounce English so well as she did. And then he told her that just as soon as she was prepared to be a teacher, he would promise to give her the best and largest girls' school in Satsuma, which is his native province, and where he is a very influential and powerful man. You can well suppose that this was a great comfort to the poor mother, a stimulus to the dear child, an encouragement to the other girls who are studying with a view to becoming teachers, and a pleasure to us, who hope, through these dear girls, to send out from this Home streams of blessings that, by God's favor, will reach the utmost bounds of this fair land.

O'Sono came to us two and a half years ago, not knowing a word of English, or even anything in her own language beyond the merest child's talk. She is now a little more than eleven years old, and is in studies quite as far advanced as most girls in American schools at that age, and reads at our morning prayers as fluently and correctly as any one in the room.

Thus you will see, my dear friends, how we are permitted to see the practical results of our interest in these children, and I trust the dear Lord will inspire in your hearts a purpose to do what you can to show your desire for the conversion of Japanese children to the Saviour, whom I trust you love and serve.

I am, most truly, your friend in Jesus,

MARY PRUYN.

XXIV.

YOKOHAMA, January 20, 1875.

MY DARLING LITTLE KITTIE:

What do you think I have to tell you now? Why, that we have a little Kittie here. Shall I tell you how this came about?

Well, to begin: a great many of the Japanese people are very poor, and they do not want any children because it costs money to feed them (not to clothe them, for not many of the poor children wear clothing), and the mother cannot work out in the field, or in any way, so well, if she has a little baby; and so a great many of these people, who are servants, but have wives, will not let any babies come to their house, because they want their wives to help them with their work.

That was the case with some of our men servants; but after they had lived here awhile, and learned that it was wicked to feel so, and that when God sent little children to them, they should be glad, and take good care of them, then they felt very differently, and became willing to let the babies come.

One of our servants, the "*belto*" (or coachman, as you would call him, for he takes care of our good old horse), was a very wicked man when he came to live with us; but he seems now a different person altogether, and I hope he is learning to love and serve our God. Last week, God sent to him and his wife a dear little girl-baby; and now that he finds what a pleasant thing it is to have one, he is just as happy as he can be; why, he can hardly bear to come out of his own little house. He says he never wants to go anywhere away from his little girl.

He feels so thankful, too, because he has such a good home and kind friends, and says he never could let a baby come before, for he had neither time nor money to care for one; and the next day after the baby was born, he came to my room, and got down on his face, as the Japanese always do when they want to be very respectful, and expressed his gratitude over and over again, for the baby, and then he said I must give her a name.

This puzzled me a little; but at last I showed him the pretty little frame that has Mary's, Bertie's, and your pictures in together, and, pointing to yours, I asked him if he would like his little girl to have the same name as that little girl who lived in America. He tried to speak the name

Kittie, and after practising a little, he found that he could pronounce it very nicely.

He was perfectly delighted, and kept saying "Arigato, Okusan," over and over again; that means "Thank you, lady;" and then he would say, "Oki Arigato;" that is, "*large* thanks."

It is a dear little baby, the prettiest Japanese child I ever saw, and has skin almost as white as yours. Some of these days I will have her picture taken and send to you, and I am sure it will please you.

Her father talks to all the ladies about his Kittie, and never gets tired of calling her name. He says, "By-and-by my Kittie go to Mrs. Peirson's school, and I hope she will be spared to grow up, and become a good and wise woman, and do a great deal of good."

And now I want you to call this your Japanese baby, and I want you to pray for her. You know God hears your prayers, for He sent you a dear little sister when you asked for her; and so you can pray for this little Japanese child, believing that God will answer you. This is all you can do now, but if she lives to be large enough to come into our school, then perhaps you can help support her.

God is very good to me in giving me so many dear little children to love, not only in my own old home, but here in this new one; and I know, too, they love me. If you were to see how they come *close* to me, and try to see how many can get within the circle of my arms, you would be amused, I think. O, if the dear Lord Jesus will make you, and them, all lambs of His fold, and guide and keep you safe from all harm and all sin, so that at last we may all gather "around the throne of God in heaven," how I will praise Him!

And now give kisses and love to all at home.

From your affectionate

GRANDMAMMA.

XXV.

YOKOHAMA, February 6, 1875.

MY DEAR MARY:

I have been reading in a book, published by an English gentleman, what is called "The Fabulous History of Japan," and as I read, I thought I would try and write it, in a very simple and plain way, for my little folks at home, so that you could understand what strange ideas these people have concerning the creation and their own origin. I may not make it very clear to you, for there is so much you could not understand which I must leave out, and perhaps that will make the story seem disconnected, or broken up; but I will do the best I can, for I like to have

my letters instructive as well as enter-
taining.

You know the Japanese, like all heathen
nations, are without the Bible, which gives
the only true account of the creation of
this world; and they must get their knowledge from tradition, or information handed
down from one to another. This kind of
information is not very reliable, for it is
so easy for different persons to change
things as they repeat them.

How much more safely we can depend
on our account of the beginning of the
world, for you know "holy men of God
spake as they were moved by the Holy
Ghost," and "all Scripture was given
by inspiration of God," and so we are
sure there is no mistake or change in our
history.

In Japanese tradition, the history of the
creation, and the descent of their emperor,

are closely connected; for "Nippon," the right name of their country, was the world to them.

They say their emperor is descended directly from the gods, and call him "The Teuno," which means "The son of heaven;" and they used to think their people were the only ones who were truly wise, and theirs the only country that was beloved and favored by the gods. This was what made them such a proud people, and so unwilling to let foreigners come among them.

The history says, anciently heaven and earth were not separated. All was mixed together in one mass, in the form of an egg; but there were two principles, or parts, in this chaos, and, after it had been agitated or shaken for a long time, the thick and heavy part settled down and became the earth, while the airy or light

part rose up, and became the heavens.
They say nothing of the creation of the
waters, though there were some, as you
will see, afterwards.

After the heavens and the earth were
thus divided, a being was born, or appeared in the heavens, called Kami, and
this they regard as the beginning of creation. But don't you see how foolish this
is? For who made the egg-shaped mass
from which the heavens and earth were
formed? And is it not much more sen-
sible and reasonable to believe what our
Bible says, "In the beginning God created
the heavens and the earth"?

After this Kami appeared, he caused to
spring up out of an island of soft mud,
that swam in the waters, a beautiful plant,
called Ashi. This was then changed into
a Kami, and he was the first of seven
celestial spirits, the three first of whom

reigned each one hundred millions of years, and all the others more years than could be counted.

Then arose a male spirit called Izanagi-no-Mikoto, and a female spirit, Izanami-no-Mikoto. They ascended to the bridge of heaven, and looking down, they said, " Are there not countries and islands down there? " Upon this they directed downward a long, heavenly spear, and stirred up the bottom of the waters.

When they drew up the spear, which was made of red precious stone, some drops of soft mud fell from it, and formed the island called Ono-koro-shima. Then these two spirits descended, and dwelt upon it; and this is the centre island of the great kingdom of the " Sunrise Land," or Dai-Nippon.

There are a great many foolish stories in this fabulous history: such as a bird coming down and beating the mud of the island hard with his tail; and how these two spirits made love to each other; how their children multiplied, and in their pride they sent one to reign in the sun, and another to be the queen of the moon; and how the first emperor of Japan came from the sun to be the ruler of their country: but I have not time to write them for you.

I have told you so much because I want you to see how far these people are from knowing the truth, and that they are to be pitied rather than blamed for not believing what they have never been taught.

Your affectionate

GRANDMAMMA.

XXVI.

June 20, 1875.

MY DEAR MARY, BERTIE, AND KITTIE:

You must not think I am always travelling because I have so much to tell you about other places than Yokohama; but I love so much to make you feel acquainted with Japan, and when I see or enjoy anything, I always feel like writing all about it to some one of the dear family at home.

Now I am going to tell you about another visit I made up on the mountains, and some of the funny things that happened there.

I have written before that we have to be carried over those mountain roads in *kagos*, and told you how very uncomforta-

ble they are for those who are not accustomed to sitting with their feet cramped up
under them, as the Japanese do.   Well, I
thought I would invent something a little
easier, and so I got a carpenter to make a
kago for me quite different, and a good
deal larger than those generally used.   It
seemed "just the very thing" for comfort,
but I did not know how strongly these
people were wedded to their old ideas
about things, or I would hardly have attempted any such experiment.

One day we made up a party to go
about ten miles off in the mountains, to
see a place that is wondrously grand and
wild, and where we had some friends
staying.   A gentleman of the party called
my *kago* the "Great Eastern," and when
I saw the others all cramped up in their
little things, and felt so comfortable in
mine, I was quite proud, and I fear a little

selfish, although I offered a good many times to let them try it.

On our way, we passed through a little village where there are a great many hot sulphur springs, and large bath-houses. There are many such places up on those mountains, and people come from all parts of Japan to get the benefit of the waters. But O, what a dreadful sight it was to see such a multitude of poor, crippled, diseased creatures together! Perhaps there is no place in the world where there are so many persons with dreadful sores all over them, as in this country; and all this is the effect of their bad way of living.

As I looked upon them, I thought of the time when Jesus was going about in Judea and Galilee, and the same kind of miserable beings crowded about Him, and asked His help in their wretchedness; "and He healed them all." O, if He were only here in Japan, what a great work He could do!

And then I thought, "No; the dear Lord is not here in His bodily presence, but He is the same loving, pitiful Saviour that He was then, and has the same power; and if these poor people only knew how to seek His help, He would surely give it."

We had not been long on the way before it began to rain, and by the time we reached Ashi-no-u, the place of the bath-houses, it just poured, and blew so hard that it was difficult for the poor coolies who were carrying us to keep on their feet. It was the harder for them because all these mountain roads are very narrow, — only a footpath, — and when a rain-storm comes, they are generally the channel, or gutter, through which the water can run off; so that the poor fellows

often could not see where they were step-
ping, but were obliged to go on blindly,
setting their feet right in the deep water,
and often on sharp stones. As they never
wear any shoes, you can think how hard
this was.

As we came near to Kiga, the place
where our friends were, the rain stopped
for a little while, for which I was very
thankful, as then we could have the large
covering of oiled paper, which prevented
our looking out over the beautiful country,
taken off, and we were able to see the
wonders and grandeur of the mountain
scenery.

The road we were on wound round the
tops of the hills till we came very near to
Kiga, and then all at once we looked
down upon the lovely little village, lying
in a valley five or six hundred feet below
us; its little straw-thatched cottages em-

bowered in the trees; its larger tea-houses, with their pleasant verandas; numerous mountain torrents, swelled by the pouring rain, dashing down in wild but glorious beauty among the rocks, — all this formed a picture that I never will forget, and the enjoyment of that scene, and the pleasant welcome we received from our friends, helped to take away from my mind the sad and painful feelings the sight at Ashi-no-u had produced.

After a good dinner, served in real foreign style, we started to return home; and then came my trial with the "Great Eastern."

Once more the rain poured down, as it only can, I think, on those mountains, and we had to be all covered and "tucked in" with oiled paper, (which, by the way, is made here in very large, soft sheets, and is used for all such purposes,) to protect

us from a drenching.   Hitherto all had
gone well with my coolies; but now they
were to show me the other side; and no
sooner did we get fairly started, than they
began: "Lady, will you give me a present?" "This *kago* very hard." "I am
very lame." "I cannot go any more."
And every few moments, setting the *kago*
on the ground, and raising the cover, they
would urge their begging for a "*sinjo*," or
present.

I did not like to give them money, for
Dr. B——, who had made all the bar-
gains with the men, had told me it was
not wise; and then I did not like to have
them see that I had a purse with me; but
as I soon found that I was far behind all
the rest of the party, I began to feel a
little nervous.

So I thought I would try something
else.   First I divided among them a pack-

age of crackers; then I tried what prom-
ises would do. "By-and-by I will give
you a *sinjo*," I said; but they would not
cease, nor go any faster, and I confess I
did begin to get a little scared, as I found
that I could no longer hear the call of the
other coolies, who were now so far away
from us. It had become very dark, and
the rain was coming down as hard as ever.
Do you wonder if my heart beat a little
faster than usual, or that I thought it just
possible there might be some serious
trouble? But I had learned something of
the character of these people, who, although very greedy because so very poor,
will not often, and then only by some
great provocation, do any real cruel thing.
So I tried to keep quiet, and asked my
dear Father to help me do just what was
best under all the circumstances.

They kept on with their importunity,

and at last I opened a basket of peaches
that I had bought at Kiga, where the finest
peaches in Japan grow, and distributed
them. It went to my heart to see them,
or rather, hear them — for it was too dark
to see anything — eating up my beautiful
peaches, that I had meant for the stay-at-
home part of our family.

All this was in vain, however, and I
had just concluded I must give them
money, when I saw a great light, and
heard the shouting of other coolies. The
rest of the party had reached Hakone, and
finding that I was not among them, had
sent their coolies back with some great
torches, made of bamboo reeds, to find
and bring my coolies home.

You may imagine how glad I was; and
when I reached my little cottage, and we
all knelt together for our evening prayers,
I thanked my dear heavenly Father for the

pleasure of the day, and for His loving care over me in my lonely ride through the storm and darkness on the mountains.

Ever your loving

GRANDMOTHER.

XXVII.

YOKOHAMA, June 27, 1875.

My dear Kittie :

I have some very sad news for you, which I am sure you will be sorry to hear.

The dear little baby, which I named after you, died two days ago. She was very sick a long time, and I fear her mother was too ignorant about babies to take good care of her. I tried to do all I could for the little thing, but all the houses in which our servants live are some way off on our large grounds, and I could not prevent the poor foolish mother from doing many things that I know were very hurtful to the child.

She had grown to be a very pretty and cunning baby, and the father and mother were so fond of her, that it was a great sorrow to them. Yet I am sure it was best, because God took her from them, and He never makes any mistakes; and then it is surely better to be in heaven with Jesus, than here in a world of sin and suffering.

I was so glad to hear, the next morning, that our good Tokichi called all our servants together, just after the baby died, and had a long talk with them, telling them what the Bible teaches about death and the resurrection of the body, and the glory and joy of heaven. Then he read what Jesus said to Martha and Mary when their brother died, and prayed with them. Was not that most beautiful in such a young Christian as he is, and one so lately ignorant of all that our precious Bible teaches?

Yesterday the heathen priest went to the house of the *belto*, and carried a picture of a god, which he put up against the side of the room; and then he told the father and mother they must pray to it, and put before it some rice and tea, and then the spirit of little Kittie would very soon go to a happy place.

After he had gone out of the house, the *belto* took the picture down and put it in the fire, and said he "never could pray to such a thing again."

Mrs. J—— and I covered a little box, and trimmed it nicely; and then I put a little white dress on the baby, and laid her in the casket we had prepared, with plenty of pretty flowers about her. She looked so sweet as she lay in her little coffin-bed, that it seemed very hard to put her away in the dark, cold ground; but then we know that just as the little seed buried in the earth springs up and bears beautiful flowers, so that little body will some day come up out of the darkness far more lovely than when it was laid away there.

We had the funeral in the school-house, and there were more than a hundred people and children present. Our school-children sang "Around the throne of God in heaven," and after the address and prayer, the whole congregation joined in singing in Japanese, "Nearer, my God, to Thee."

It is so pleasant to feel that by all these circumstances our dear children are being taught some good lessons. I think little Kittie's death will be the means by which a good many will learn of a better life in heaven, and that we need not be afraid to die, if we only love and trust Jesus.

Are you not glad that there is a Home where these poor heathen people and children can hear the "good news"?

And now I want to tell you and Mary, and Bertie too, for I think he worked hard for the Fair, as well as the girls, that the money you sent me I used to buy two little bedsteads, and the beds and pillows for them.

I wish I could draw a picture of the room in which they stand. There were four little beds in it, but we needed more very badly, so now we have them, six in all, and two little girls sleep in each one. They stand in a square, right in the middle of the room, three on one side, and three on the other, with the heads together. This seems a queer way, perhaps, to you, but it gives better air, we think, to all the little sleepers, and it is easier to get around the room.

I wish you could see how comfortable and cunning they all look. I think you would feel well paid for all your hard work for the Fair.

But now I cannot write any more, only to say that I am, just as I always will be,
Your loving

GRANDMA.

XXVIII.

KATASI, JAPAN, August 2, 1875.

DEAR CHILDREN:

Shut up this rainy morning in a little Japanese house, with a group of restless but playful children about me, it is not very easy to write; yet I think I must try and have some talk with a few of the dear little ones far away in America, who are so much interested in our Home and children. I can tell them how a part of our family are spending a portion of the vacation, and what there is here for little people to enjoy in a cheap and quiet way.

I felt sorry for the nine children of our family who had no home to go to during our vacation, and so, after a good deal of thought as to what we could do for them, I concluded to go somewhere off in the country, where they could have a change of air and scene. It was quite a difficult thing for me to do, for you know I cannot talk Japanese at all, and the people in the country know nothing of English. And besides, several of these children have not yet learned to speak or understand it either. However, I felt quite sure our dear Father would help me in thus trying to give pleasure to others, and He has done it wonderfully in so many ways since I came away from our Home, that my heart is full of praise every hour. I find in trying to make others happy I had the largest share of blessing myself.

This place where we are staying is on the sea-shore, and right opposite, and connected by a long, sandy beach, or neck, washed up by the sea, is the sacred island of Inoshima. That is a great place of resort in the summer, for foreigners and pilgrims, who go in great crowds to visit the numerous shrines in the island, and celebrated cave under it, where there are so many gods for them to worship that I could not attempt to count them.

It would not be wise for us to be in such a public place; but here, in this little village, we have all the pleasure of the sea-shore, and can walk over to the island whenever we desire. I wish I could give you a picture of this pretty little Japanese house. Not the outside, for that does not look very pretty with its unpainted and black boards, and heavy straw-thatched roof; but the inside part, which we occupy, is all new and clean, and so cunning, with its nice mats on the floor and white paper doors, which slide any way we like, and with which we can make our rooms large

or small, just as we choose. Our rooms
are built apart from the rest of the house,
and all around them there is a small veranda. On this and upon the mats in the
room, people can step with their shoes
on, and I really think there is nothing our
children enjoy more than going about here
barefooted. Is not that just like all children in hot weather? and do you wonder
that these little ones are glad to do just
what they always used to do before they
came to our house, namely, run about barefooted, and sleep on the mats? Well, it
certainly is nice for a little while in such
warm weather; but when we get back to
our own home, it will not be good for those
whom we hope will become intelligent
young ladies, and help to teach their people to live a civilized life, like the ladies
of Christian lands.

Yesterday we got a boat, and went

around the island of Inoshima. It is just like an immense rock thrown up by some terrible earthquake out of the water. Its sides are all ragged and broken in a fearful way, and down near the bottom are numberless little caves. We ventured to go into but one of these caves, for the tide and the currents make it too dangerous; but in the large one, where the shrines for so many gods have been made, every one wants to go and see the wonderful place: I did not think it safe for our little ones to go in, and they were quite satisfied to do just what I thought best.

One day we got a boat, and went along up the shore about three miles, to Kamakura, to see the great bronze idol of Diabutz. This is one of the largest and oldest idols in the world, and it is one of the places where every one who comes to Japan always desires to go. So you see our children can see a good deal that is very interesting, even in coming to this little country village. Every day they go down to the beach and bathe in the delightful surf that rolls in from the great Pacific Ocean. The bathing is real fun and pleasure for them, and they have always been so accustomed to such things, that it does not trouble them that there are no bath-houses and conveniences for undressing and dressing. I must say that for me it is *not* pleasant, though I try to make a tent of my umbrella beside the *jinrikisha*, which we take to carry the two little ones and the bathing-suits; for the sand is so deep that only the larger girls can manage to get through it, over the hills washed up all along the beach.

The old man who keeps this house is very fond of children, and always goes with us and takes care of the little ones;

and sometimes when I see how happy he is with them around him, I think our coming here will make a brighter spot in his life, as well as theirs. A few days ago he fixed up some bamboo rods, and took them all out to fish; and though, like many wiser and older anglers, they came home with very few prizes, yet they were as much pleased as if their baskets were full.

I am sure you would be glad to hear our little girls sing for these people, and I told them that was the very best way for them to be little missionaries here. They can sing some of our sweet hymns that have been translated into Japanese; and when I hear them singing, in a language those about them can understand, "I am so glad that our Father in Heaven," "I am Jesus' Little Lamb," and so many hymns that tell the "sweet story" we love so well, I lift up my heart in secret prayer, that in this way some seed may be sown in this dark place, that will take root and bear some fruit for the glory of God.

In two days more we will go home again, and spend the rest of the vacation there; but I am sure these dear little girls will be better and happier for this visit, and I hope you will pray that the people who have heard them sing, and seen them kneel every morning and evening to pray to the true God, will not forget, but desire to know more of our Home and the religion we teach there; for this is one of the ways in which we hope to send out streams of blessing that shall reach many corners of this land.

Ever your loving friend,

MARY PRUYN.

XXIX.

YOKOHAMA, August 29, 1875.

MY DEAR LITTLE FOLKS AT HOME:

I am sitting down to write you a few lines, which will be my last letter from Japan. Although I long so much to see you, and must look forward with joy to the prospect of being once more in the dear old home, yet it is with the keenest pain that I have at last decided to leave this precious new home.

You have heard of my ill health, so long continued that it seems now necessary for me to go away into some other climate, and so I have no choice but to do just as the dear Lord directs.

I cannot write you any more from Japan, but I hope the letters I have written, and all you have heard about this country and our school, have been carefully remembered, and that you will continue to feel an interest in the work here.

You must not think because grandmamma leaves these dear children, you can forget them, or cease to do all you can for their education.

This Home and school are now fairly established, and God has most wonderfully blessed all our labor here; but if this work is to go on, as it surely ought, and grow larger and more useful every year, then all the dear friends in America must continue to help it.

I only send these few lines to tell you that I shall expect you to love and work for Japan as long as there is anything you can do.

And now, in closing this my last letter to the dear little folks, I want them all to carry out the sentiment of the following sweet lines, which Miss M. G. Brainard has, at my request, kindly written expressly for them : —

> Lambs of Jesus, guarded, sheltered,
>   By the Shepherd good and true,
> Eating of His greenest pasture,
>   Drinking in His sweetest dew, —
>   There are others
>   Who might eat and drink with you.
>
> Far off on the darkest mountains,
>   Little lambs are wandering bold,
> Knowing not there is a shelter,
>   Knowing not there is a Fold,
>   And a Shepherd
>   Who would shield them from the cold.
>
> Send some word of pity to them,
>   Saying to the wanderers, " Come,
> Let our Shepherd be your Shepherd,
>   — There can never be but One, —
>   Let one Sheepfold
>   Be our everlasting Home."

Your loving

GRANDMOTHER.